ISBN 978-0-9928012-1-2

This first paperback edition printed by CreateSpace

THE ADVENTURES OF TRAVELLER TIM

By Roy Young

Youngs Books

Acknowledgements

To Carol whose patience and enthusiasm have never waned;
Mark Chisnell for his thoughts and guidance; to Charlotte,
Matthew, Trevor, Gary and Lesley for all their help in teaching
me new computer skills; and finally to Frances Clarke for
bringing it all together and making this book possible.

Written by R.W.YOUNG

Illustrated by Amy Lyons

**This book is dedicated to
MARIA**

Table Of Contents

Chapter 1. Deal's Done

Tim's dad walked past the hen house, scuffing his heels in the dried earth.

"Fed them chickens yet?"

Troosh, the big Alsatian, twitched his ears but remained lying down.

"Just about to"

Tim jumped up from where he had been sitting, leaning against some straw bales, day dreaming as usual. He often sat staring into space, letting his mind run wild, trying to live out his daydreams about stories he had read. This time he was on his travels around the world in eighty days, sailing across the large blue ocean in a beautiful sailing ship with a full head of sail. Porpoises were breaking the surface of the water as the bow dipped and rose from the sea. He was brought back to reality by his dad, muttering under his breath as he headed back to their caravan.

"You need a kick up the backside sometimes."

Tim picked up an old pail. It was going a bit rusty on the outside and there was much squeaking on the handle as he swung it to and fro. He walked towards the old railway carriages, now devoid of their wheels and resting on some old sleepers. Tim pulled at the vertical bar which ran the full height of the door, and the door creaked along its runners letting in shafts of light, dust rising from the floor like a misty cloud with sunlight picking out the gossamer thread of the cobwebs. Adjusting his eyes to the dim light he entered. Inside was an assortment of bins of animal feed: corn for the chickens, mill for the young pigs and some supplement for the goats. Tim picked the scoop from the floor and half filled his bucket with corn. Back outside, he slid the door shut so as to keep out unwanted visitors of the rodent kind.

Walking back towards the hen house he began swinging the bucket and shaking the corn about.

"Here, chick chicks, here, chick chicks," he called.

The hens came running from all corners of the smallholding; scampering to meet him as he served them a mid morning snack. Tim grabbed handfuls of corn and with a swing of his arm broadcast it evenly across the ground. The hens stooped down to peck away at the corn just as though they were clockwork toys. He emptied the remainder, placing the bucket up-side down on the ground next to the hen house to keep it dry. Mooching along, Tim then went looking for the day's eggs. He knew all the odd places that the hens would lay. Holding his tee-shirt up at the front he wandered around picking

up all the eggs; small ones from the bantams and larger ones from the chickens; placing them in the pouch that the tee-shirt formed.

Tim was nearly fourteen, tall for his age and starting to fill out. He had a small scar to the left side of his chin which came about when he caught it on some barbed wire as he tried to jump a fence while being chased by a farmer for nicking apples. His shiny mop of brown hair flowed down to his collar and two dimples appeared in his cheeks when he smiled, which was often.

Tim's mum had passed away, when he was seven, dying from a lung disease which she had suffered from as a young girl. Seeing his mother bedridden was a traumatic time in Tim's life. He did not fully understand why relatives were fussing over her. Of course they had been trying to make her last days as bearable as possible. When she passed away there was great sadness; sobbing and crying and the women wailing. But where was his dad, Sean? The word had gone out to locate him amongst the travelling community for until he returned the funeral could not take place. It was a week after she died that Sean finally returned bleary eyed through lack of sleep, unshaven, looking distraught and seeking his son. A caravan door burst open and Tim had lunged out, running towards his father, his eyes welling tears. Sean stretched out his arms to receive his son as he jumped up. They clung together tightly. Tim's welling tears turned to crying. He was so pleased to see his dad, yet so angry and frustrated that his dad had not been there. His hands became clenched fists and he turned white with rage. With his arms raised, his fists started to pummel down on Sean's shoulders harder and harder.

"Where were you, where were you?" He screamed.

This just made Sean cling to him even more.

"You're never here! We needed you, and Mum needed you!"

Tim was now kicking. His whole body became frantic. Relaxing his grip Sean lowered Tim down.

"I hate you, I hate you," cried Tim. And with one last kick he turned and ran into the arms of one of his aunties.

Sean sank to his knees with his head in his hands, for he loved his son more than life itself. He knew then, that one day, bridges would have to be built over these troubled waters.

*

Tim was brought up by a succession of aunties and family friends. Tim's favourite auntie was his mum's sister, Auntie Elsie. She spent a lot of time with him teaching him to read and write. She kept telling him about the advantages he would have over others who, like his dad, couldn't be bothered to read and write. She was a softly spoken and cuddly kind of auntie, round faced with rosy red cheeks, always a smile on her face. She was never without her apron and her hands had skin that looked like leather because of all the hard work she had done. Even though she had five children of her own, Tim was never left out, and deep down she always had a soft spot for Sean.

Back in those days Sean was nearly always out on the road - tarmacing drives, hedge cutting, tree felling, almost anything that would earn him some money. Then when Tim reached the age of eleven, Sean acquired a piece of land, just over three acres in all, bordered on one side by a stream which was spring fed and overhung by two weeping willows. Though Sean didn't want to be tied down, for he was a free spirit, he decided that it would be good for Tim to have somewhere he could call home.

As Sean had worked and schemed and saved all his life he had the money to buy the land. He never trusted banks, always believing cash is king, and he had many biscuit tins, cake tins and an old tobacco jar stuffed with bank notes and hidden under the bench seats of the caravan. One day, as Tim sat on his dad's bunk, Sean took out all the tins of money and between them they started to empty their contents. One lid was so tight Tim had to get a spoon to prise it loose. He sat open mouthed looking in astonishment as the pile of paper money grew and grew, more money than he had ever seen in his life. Tim ran his fingers through it and grabbing hold of a large handful he threw it up into the air. It all weaved and floated down.

"Look, Dad," he shouted. "It's raining ten pound notes!"

And they both fell about laughing.

After they had composed themselves they set about picking up all the money, sorting it into piles of five, ten and twenty pound notes, and counting. As we know, Sean could not read or write and relied on Tim. Sometimes this annoyed Tim and it caused frequent arguments. But where money was concerned Sean had no problem. The piles of notes grew taller on the bedspread.

"That's the lot; all we possess, Son."

Tim with pencil in hand and a scrap of paper started totalling up the columns.

"We have a grand total of…" he paused, "two thousand six hundred and forty five pounds. How much do we need to buy the land?"

"Twelve hundred quid," replied his dad.

"That's an awful lot."

"Don't worry son, it's all for us and we can always earn some more and now we will have something to show for our hard work."

Sean wasn't too sure of himself but tried to sound convincing.

They bundled up the money they needed and set off in the pick-up truck. The truck was old and tatty, rusting in parts. The back tail gate was held in place with bailing twine. An old coat hanger served instead of the aerial which had long been broken off. The front bench seat was covered with an old blanket as the original covers had been rubbed away. They reached their destination, turning into a farm track overgrown on both sides with tall grasses and stinging nettles. It led them to a bungalow. Sean stopped, pulled on the hand brake but left the vehicle in gear, seeing as the hand brake did not work very well. He turned off the engine and they both got out. Tim went round to join his dad.

Outside the open front door of the bungalow stood a short plump fellow in clothes that had never seen an iron. The garments were dreadfully creased and crumpled. The man had no collar to his shirt and the buttons were done up in the wrong holes. One hand was in his trouser pocket while the other twiddled a matchstick in the corner of his mouth.

"Morning, Edmond," said Sean.

"Morning."

Edmond walked down the steps from his bungalow. He still had his slippers on. One of his toes was sticking out.

"Shall we get down to business?" said Sean.

"Got the money?" enquired Edmond.

"Sure thing."

Sean reached into his pocket and pulled out a wad of notes, offering them. Edmond withdrew his hand from his pocket to take the money, and then proceeded to count it.

"Don't worry, it's all there," remarked Sean.

"I believe you, just checking. Hate for you to give me too much!" said Edmond sarcastically.

At this, Tim took an instant dislike to him.

"You're right," said Edmond, "it's all there. OK. I'll have all the necessary paperwork for you later this week and in the meantime here's a receipt."

He gave Sean a scribbled receipt as he stuffed the money in his pocket with the other hand. Tim took the piece of paper off his dad and checked it, to ensure all was in order.

"OK, deal's done let's shake on it."

Sean raised his hand to his mouth, spitting into the palm of his hand. Edmond did the same and the two men joined hands taking a firm grip and shook vigorously. Then Tim and his dad turned their backs, got into their pick-up and drove off with Edmond still stood in his drive way.

"I don't like him very much, Dad, he's a bit slimy."

"I know what you mean, Son but he's not a bad sort. When this piece of land first came up, all hell broke loose when the locals found out about me wanting to buy it. They didn't want a traveller getting his hands on it for fear of the trouble it might cause and lowering the tone of the neighbourhood. When Edmond heard this it made him all the more determined to sell to me, so I say good on him."

Chapter 2. Dunroamin

That was almost three years ago, they are now the proud owners of their piece of Paradise; something they both thought would never happen. But every time Sean looks at Tim and sees how happy the boy is he knows he did the right thing.

On their plot of land they have a forty-two foot caravan and over the door hangs a sign cut from an oak log and suspended by two chains, which reads: "DUNROAMIN" with the letters chiselled deep and painted red. They managed to barter for the caravan. Sean had seen it up for sale on a local caravan site while driving around looking for work, so a deal was struck: if both father and son worked, helping the owner of the caravan site clear and tidy up the site, they could have the caravan for free. However, this wasn't as good as it sounds for it took them three weeks of hard graft to satisfy the owner. Once the man was satisfied, he arranged delivery.

Backing the lorry down their drive took a few attempts as it had some awkward twists and turns but eventually it was done and they got the caravan blocked up and level. Inside it they have two spacious bedrooms with plenty of storage space, a big lounge where the settee folds down to make an extra bed should any visitors wish to stay over, a fitted kitchen compact but workable, a small gas stove and a gas fridge. The shower room is a bit cramped though it serves its purpose

At first, all the lights were run off a bank of car batteries but eventually they got a diesel generator. This isn't as good as mains electricity for boiling the kettle or having a shower because it drains the power and the lights go dim. When it is winter time and dark early, blowing a gale, it's no fun for Sean and Tim having to go outside to top up the diesel, but nonetheless, for them it's a great way of life. They don't have a television but that never bothered Tim because he loves books and is often found with his nose buried in one.

Outside the caravan, between the pair of them they rigged up electrical cables running from the small shed they erected around the generator, to the four railway carriages still painted dark brown from the days when British Rail used them, and the lean-to which kept their logs dry for their fire. Other sheds they built, were made from old pallets and scrap timber covered in corrugated iron sheets. These didn't have lights as there was not enough power, so the pair used a torch if needed, to go to them in the dark.

Tim made the kennel for Troosh out of some old pallets that had been discarded at the side of the road. The name, Troosh, means, 'to frighten someone' in Cant, the language used by the older generation of travelling people. Auntie Elsie had taught Tim to speak Cant and he can still remember most of it. The kennel had an old flour sack nailed over the opening to keep out the worst of the weather. Troosh had a cosy bed on a thick layer of straw which Tim changed every week. A choker chain, secured onto a long running line, allowed the dog to run up and down alongside the caravan and sheds. Troosh is never allowed into the caravan but when Tim and his dad are around they let him off the wire to roam free. An assortment of cats inhabits the plot, all wild. Some are black and white, one is tortoiseshell and two are ginger. They sleep anywhere they can that is warm and dry and out of Troosh's way. Sean is not so keen on the cats and sometimes has a falling out with them. Tim hears cussing and then a bang and crash as Sean hurls a brick in their direction and the cats scatter to find a hiding place. The cats earn their keep because they keep down the rats and mice.

Over time, Father and son have divided up their smallholding with fencing, making small paddocks. They have three goats; two nannies and a Billy; which, when not in their paddock, are tethered by means of a chain and a stake driven into the ground which is moved every so often to give them fresh grass. It's Tim's job to milk the nannies every day but the Billy goat he avoids, for if you turn your back on him, and if he is so inclined, he will butt you and send you flying.

Then there are the pigs. About every three months or so, Sean and Tim go off to market on a Tuesday and buy six weaners. These live in their makeshift shelter to be fattened up before being sold. Every so often it is time to swap the pens around due to the way the pigs turn over the soil. Sean calls them 'God's little ploughs'.

Seeing as they have no freezer, Sean has made a deal with Mick, the local butcher, whereby he gives Mick two of the pigs, and they call in at Mick's anytime they want and collect meat or bacon. Mick gets half a pig for himself for his trouble. The other pigs get sold to friends and family. This pays for any straw or feed they need. Sometimes in the summer when the local hotels and pubs are busy, Sean and Tim drive around and collect the swill (left over food which is being thrown away) and bring it back to feed to their pigs. Often they find knives and forks in with the swill because somebody has been too lazy to sort them. Even the odd plate or two has turned up.

In some of the sheds and stacked around their land are piles of scrap and what might seem like discarded rubbish. Sean never throws anything away saying, "It's all worth something to somebody, at some time, so let's keep it, till that some when."

Spring and summer are the best times. Tim really enjoys those times of year. He spends as much time outside as he can, playing inside a camp he made in one of the piles of scrap, or lying on top of the hen house in his shorts reading a book. His pride and joy is an old Morris Minor van which his dad collected from somewhere. In this, Tim has driven all over the country with Troosh by his side, touring up hills and down dales. He even entered the Le Mans race and won! Only in his dreams of course. In reality this is impossible because he is too young and can't drive, and his dad removed the engine and gearbox and sold them!

*

One morning, at the beginning of April, spring was in full force. The weather had been very mild for the time of year and wild flowers were emerging from beneath the undergrowth in the hedgerows, wild pansies showing their array of colours with bright painted faces, the only flower to smile back at you. Hawthorn was sprouting new shoots and Tim liked to nibble on these new shoots as hawthorn in some parts is called the bread and cheese plant. This particular morning Tim was helping his dad load up the empty gas bottles into the back of the pick-up. They used bottle gas for cooking and some of their heating so this was one of the chores they had to do every now and then; part of living in the country. Once ready to set off, Tim hitched up Troosh to his wire, and then walked down the drive to open the gate. His dad drove through and Tim slammed the gate closed and hopped into the pick-up. To get out of their place they had to drive down a narrow track, fenced on both sides to stop Edmond's cattle getting out. Another 'Dunroamin' sign hung by the entrance to their place and under that they had built a small box on legs. Any surplus eggs they had were put there to be sold by the half dozen, with an honesty box for the money. No post was ever delivered and no postman would go near Troosh.

Turning left they headed for the small village of Waltonson and not far down the road they were soon pulling onto the forecourt of the garage. It was no grand affair, the building just made of timber and painted blue with enamel signs nailed to its exterior. There was one petrol pump, one diesel pump and a paraffin pump up against the wall. The front shop had a counter with a cash register on it. A glass case, with some sweets laid out, stood in the corner and motor spares were hanging sparsely around the walls. A few had a thick layer of dust, evidence of how long they had hung there, unused.

Sean started to unload the five empty gas bottles then stood them up against the workshop wall.

The garage owner, Joe Maxwell, was a genius with anything mechanical. No matter what the problem, he could sort it out.

"Here, Sean, let me give you a hand," came his voice. Joe emerged from his workshop, wiping his hands on an oily rag.

"Cheers mate."

Sean started to load the new bottles onto the pick-up.

To look at Joe you wouldn't think he had the muscle to lift heavy gas bottles. He rose no more than five feet four inches from the ground, his boiler suit hung like rags on a scarecrow and he had hair that went around his head just above his ears with nothing on the top except a few grease marks where he had been working under a car. His advanced years had left him with a slight stoop.

"Fancy a cuppa?" he said.

"Don't mind if I do." Sean secured the tail gate "You'd better give us a couple of pints of oil for the old girl, Joe."

"Right oh."

Sitting in the workshop, on empty, five-gallon oil drums, the two men, mugs of tea in hand, exchanged small talk. Watching Joe hitting the side of his mug with his spoon Tim realised just why all of Joe's cups had chips around the top. He went outside to amuse himself by rooting around in the rubbish and scrap. He could see that spying out of the murky window; Sean was keeping an eye on him. Their voices floated out through the open door.

"I'll take that lot off your hands if you like." Sean nodded in the direction of the scrap.

Joe took a swig of tea. "You might as well. The place could do with a tidy up."

"How's does this afternoon sound?"

"Yes whenever you like. By the way Sean, I'm looking for a rear axle for a fifty eight Morris and a bonnet too. D'you happen to know where I might get one?"

"I might. What's it worth?" teased Sean, sensing a deal.

"Tell you what; you get me the axle and the bonnet along with the mounting plates and you can have the oil, the gas bottles and the scrap in exchange. How's that sound?"

"You've got a deal, you'll have them today. Must dash; I've got a lot to do." Sean rose and put his empty cup on Joe's workbench.

Outside he called Tim whose head just showed over the steering wheel as he sat in Joe's breakdown truck. Tim jumped down to join his dad. On the way home Sean told him of the deal he had struck with Joe.

"But Dad that's my Morris," said Tim pleading with his dad not to cannibalise it any more.

"Sorry Son, business is business."

Tim, with a scowl on his face, sat in stony silence for the rest of the journey home. Getting out of the pick-up he swung the door shut so hard that it shook the whole vehicle. He walked over and opened the gate. His dad ignored him and drove through. Closing the gate Tim walked up to the caravan where his dad was now unloading the gas bottles.

"Come on, cheer up, Lad" said his dad "Let's get moving."

Tim forced a smile on his face and went off to get some tools and jacks from inside one of the sheds. He rejoined his dad and they headed for the Morris.

"Pull those blocks over."

Tim pulled over some concrete blocks and laid them either side of the wheels. His dad slid the jacks under the van. With the wheel nuts loosened, the van started to rise. Within an hour the two of them had the axle off and loaded in the pick-up. The bonnet was white with chicken muck with just the odd patch or two of green showing through. They released it and loaded and tied it down. Then they were heading back to Joe's. Driving round the back, Sean pulled up just as Joe was throwing an old exhaust pipe on the pile of scrap.

"Didn't take you long," said Joe.

"You know me, Joe; I can always lay my hands on most things."

The two men unloaded the spare parts from the pick-up and put them in the workshop.

"This will please old Maude," said Joe, "she'll be able to have her old car back now, and it's her baby, she's had it since it was new, but I'm not sure about the chicken muck." Joe rubbed his chin.

Sean reversed the pick-up back to where the pile of scrap lay. Before long all was loaded and fitted in like a jigsaw. There was no more room even to fit one more piece on. The springs at the back were bent flat and the front wheels were almost off the ground but with Tim and his dad aboard, the pick-up settled down.

Off they headed with blue smoke belching out at the back, driving like the clappers and swaying all across the road, trying to get to Collins scrap yard before it closed. They made it, taking the sharp right hand turn into Collins yard very gingerly so as not to turn the pick-up over.

"All mixed?" asked the man, from his small booth.

"Aye." Sean struggled to wind down the window.

"Onto the weigh bridge please and get out."

They complied with the man's instruction. Once weighed they got back in and drove down alongside the towering sheds. Unloading was a lot quicker. They dragged it all off; the old exhaust pipe and silencers, wheels, bent and twisted body panels and a couple of gear boxes. When their task was complete, Sean drove back onto the weigh bridge, then getting out he received his ticket from the gentleman, and walking over to the pay office he handed it in.

A rude woman grabbed the ticket and promptly turned her back and walked away. Having worked out the weight of the scrap she then used a calculator to work out what was owed.

"Here you go, sign here," she barked coming over to the window hatch.

Sean, who couldn't write, took the pen dangling on a piece of string and scribbled something illegible. The woman then went over to unlock the money drawer to extract cash, counting out some notes.

"There you are, twenty one pounds," she said, then closed the hatch before Sean could say a word.

Back home with all the animals fed and sorted they headed into the caravan. Tim made a cup of tea and some sandwiches for them both.

"There you go, Son, not bad for a day's work. Free oil and gas bottles and a few quid in our pockets. I can't wait to see what tomorrow brings."

Chapter 3. Tim gets a soaking

On their land was a fresh water spring and, once a week, father and son went down to it, rigging up hose pipes for their supply of water. Sean had built up some concrete blocks into piers. On top was a large galvanised tank with a sheet of plywood as a lid and a tarpaulin draped over it, secured on the side of the shed. Just below the tank was a hand rotary pump. Tim laid out the connected hose pipes to the spring whilst Sean secured the other end onto the pump with a jubilee clip. Tim then filled a large jam jar with water and poured this into the top of the pump to prime it.

"Alright lad, pump away" called out Sean.

With Tim pumping away at the handle, water was pulled along the pipe and up into the tank. In turn the water in the tank fed along a series of pipes to their caravan and also an outside tap and to automatic drinkers for some of the animals.

"Dad, are you going to take over now? My arms are really aching" said Tim, sweat running from his brow.

"Ok Son, give us it here."

Sean took hold of the handle and continued pumping away from side to side. Tim sat down for a rest. Soon the tank was full and water came out of the hole at the top which was used for the overflow, cascading down all over Tim as he sat on the ground.

"Arghh Dad!"

Tim jumped up and shook himself.

"You were overdue a bath."

His dad was laughing his head off. Even Troosh thought it was funny, wagging his tail and barking. Tim went into the caravan to get dried off and change his clothes. Mick the local butcher was arriving soon to pick up the pigs.

Mick arrived and reversed his trailer up to the gate where the pigs were housed, ready to take them to the abattoir.

As Tim came out to join them his dad told Mick about the soaking and the two men had a laugh at Tim's expense.

Mick was a shy man who wore a white coat, a blue stripped apron and a white cap. There was always a pencil behind his ear. Eager to get on, he dropped the ramp to his trailer and positioned hurdles from there to the gate.

Sean jumped into the pen with a piece of ply board. Tim opened the five bar gate and Sean got behind the pigs and drove them forward. Slowly the animals edged towards the ramp controlled by Sean's waving arms and whistling. When the pigs were in the back of the trailer, Mick swung the trailer gates closed and raised up the ramp locking it into place.

"Catch up with you later."

Mick jumped back into his van and drove off.

"Quick cup of tea, Son?"

"I'll put the kettle on" offered Tim.

It was such a lovely afternoon that they sat outside, each eating a lump of cake with their mugs of tea. Troosh waited, eager to lick up the crumbs.

"There's still plenty of daylight left so let's set too with the mucking out shall we?"

"If we must," Tim sighed.

This wasn't the best of jobs but when you have animals there's not any choice, so taking a wheelbarrow each, and a pitch fork, they set about their task. Filling their wheelbarrows with straw and animal droppings from the pens, they walked down to the bottom of their land to pile it on top of the already rotting manure. Edmond used to come round with his tractor and trailer to collect it all, every so often, and then he'd spread it over his land for fertilizer. Within a few days the whole pile would be gone and the patch cleaned and disinfected. Then Sean and Tim dug the ground over.

For now, with the mucking out complete, they put new straw in the sty ready for the next batch of pigs. Later they collected their money from Mick along with a joint of meat for their weekend treat. Even after taking out the money for their next batch of weaners, along with feed and straw, they were still in profit by just over twenty seven pounds.

"Not bad for a couple of old travellers," said Sean, rubbing Tim's head in affection, as they headed back into the caravan. "Wish your Ma could be here now, I think she'd be proud of us."

Sean went over to the picture on the sideboard. Lifting it up, he rubbed the silver frame with the sleeve of his shirt. "If only," he muttered.

"If only, what Dad?"

"Oh, nothing to worry yourself about, Son."

Tim knew that his dad had loved his mum very much and he never showed any interest in getting married again, even with the combined attempts at match making from his aunties.

Chapter 4. New loo

Sean one day decided that it was about time they had a proper toilet. There was one, in their caravan, but it had never been connected to any system which would allow them to flush it. The one they were using was outside - a small shed over a deep hole with a plank of wood for a seat. In the corner was a bucket of wood shavings and a scoop and every so often they would sprinkle some down the hole. Their toilet paper was newspaper cut into squares and threaded on a piece of string and hung on a rusty nail. In the height of summer it could hum a bit so they were in and out a quick as possible.

So Sean did a deal with his brother, Jim, wherein their part of the deal was to go and help Jim with some tarmacing. On the way to the site, Sean stopped off to buy a dozen packets of peppermints.

"What are those for Dad?" asked Tim, "can I have one?"

"No you can't, those are for something special," said his dad mysteriously. "You'll see."

The job was at a large elegant house and there they all met up. Jim went to the front door and rang the bell. As the door edged open, there stood a city gent looking smart in a crisp white shirt, tie and a clean-cut pinstriped suit. He wore highly polished shoes you could see your face in.

"Morning guv," Jim greeted him.

"Oh, good morning. Everything is ready for you, I'll just move my car out of the way, don't want any grubby hands all over it."

The man's voice sounded as though he was talking with a load of gob stoppers in his mouth. He was looking down his nose at them as though they were second class citizens. Tim could concede that maybe they weren't the smartest of folk but he knew very well that they were never afraid of hard work.

The job was not difficult. The drive had already been tarmaced some years ago but was now looking tired and scruffy. They set to, filling in the pot holes and cleaning up the edges. Sean was on the rake because he had a good eye for levelling out the hot tarmac. Jim was in charge, so he took care of the rolling. That left Tim and his cousin Sonny, shovelling the tarmac from the back of Jim's transit, where it was kept covered by a thick sheet to keep the heat in. Sonny, who was a year older than Tim, had earrings in both ears and wore three gold chains around his neck. The two lads barrowed the hot black tarmac into the drive-way. Occasionally Sean would stop and wipe their tools and the roller with a cloth soaked in diesel, to prevent the tarmac from sticking. Soon it was all laid and raked and Jim walked back and forth, rolling it and switching the roller from one hand to the other.

Once they had stopped shovelling, it was Tim's job to clear up while Sonny operated the hand thumper, tapping down the edges where the roller couldn't reach. Sean returned to the pick-up and retrieved the peppermints from the cab. Placing them in a large paper bag he proceeded to hit them with a lump of wood, breaking them up into finer fragments, then delving into the bag and taking a hand full, he scattered them over the newly laid drive way. With one final roll the job was done. The city gent came out to inspect their work.

"Hmmm, yes, yes," he said walking up and down the drive. "Fine job, and my idea of having the white bits just sets it off. Here's your money."

He handed Jim a brown envelope.

"Ta," Jim replied, lifting the flap of the envelope. "Glad you're pleased with the job."

He thumbed through the notes.

"Those white bits may fade in time," he added.

Jim was clearly having to work really hard to keep a straight face. He stuffed the envelope into his back pocket and they collected their tools and loaded up. Climbing into the cab they went on their way with howls of laughter.

They stopped off at Jim's place next, where they hitched the trailer (which was already loaded with a small digger) to the transit. It was time to do Jim's part of the deal.

They drove to Dunroamin where they off-loaded the digger and Sonny jumped on to it, turning the key to rev it into life. White smoke erupted from the exhaust pipe. Sonny pulled on the levers and it spun around then slowly trundled along on its tracks.

They dug a trench from the outside toilet back to the caravan, and Jim and Sean laid in the four-inch drainage pipes. Once they had coupled everything together and joined it to the toilet in the caravan, Sonny back filled the trench and tamped it down with the digger bucket. Manoeuvring back, he continued the trench in the other direction, all the way to the boundary fence, connecting up with Edmond's cesspit tank. Once the final pipes were laid and back filled, Sonny steered the digger back onto the trailer.

"Who's going to christen it first?" Said Sean.

"Me, Dad, I'm bursting." Tim rushed forward.

"No more putting on our wellies and raincoats to take a leak," said Sean. "Some of life's simplest things, we take for granted."

The two brothers shook hands and they settled down to relax in the caravan, drinking a few cans of beer and reminiscing about the old days and their travels. They had travelled a lot together in the past, working and enjoying life out on the open road. Jim had been a bare knuckle fighter and when the fairs were in towns the brothers used to roll up and look for the posters that proclaimed: "If you last three rounds, you win ten pounds." Jim used to do quite well though he lost more than he won, which was why he now had a cauliflower ear and a nose that looked like it was made of rubber because it had been broken so many times he could squash it into any shape. Now that they had settled down with their own families the brothers didn't see quite so much of each other.

Next morning Sean was up and about early. He fed the animals and milked the goats. Troosh was let off his chain and chased around the yard after the cats.

As Sean came back into the caravan, he met Tim rubbing his eyes.

"Morning Dad."

"Morning, Son, how's you this fine day?"

Tim was still half asleep. He slipped his coat and shoes on and was just about to head outside.

"Off somewhere?" queried Sean.

"Just going to the loo."

"What's the matter with using the one in here?"

"Eh?"

Tim stopped in his tracks and engaged his brain.

"Oh yes."

He kicked off his shoes, slipped the coat from his shoulders and threw it on the chair, heading into the bathroom. After a few minutes he returned into the lounge.

"Awake now are we?"

"Yes Dad."

"Should have let you go off out there."

"Funny ha ha," said Tim going over to the cupboard to get some cereal for his breakfast, noticing his dad had already got the milk.

"When you've had that, meet me down the bottom of the yard."

Chomping on his cereal Tim raised his hand, unable to speak as his mouth was full.

Sean went down to where they stored the straw for the animals. Gathering up all the loose straw he could find he went over to the old outside toilet. Opening the door he stepped back as the smell reached his nostrils. He stuffed all the loose straw inside. Closing the door for the last time he left some straw sticking out, and then collecting up other bits of rubbish, he leaned them up against the timber frame of the little shed.

"What's doing Dad?"

Tim arrived on the scene tucking his shirt into his trousers. His dad took a box of matches from his jacket pocket.

"Here, Son, you can have the honours."

He threw the matches. Tim caught the box. Approaching the old toilet door he took out a single match. He struck and it flared into life. Bending down Tim put the flame to the dry straw and flames slowly rose into the air followed by a column of dense smoke. They both stood back as the fire took hold, flames dancing higher and higher, the wood spitting and cracking in the intense heat.

"Am I pleased to see that go," remarked Tim as they both retreated further. The timber structure, now slowly twisting, fell to the ground. Sparks and burning embers rose skyward.

"OK, let's collect all the rubbish that's lying around," said Sean.

They headed off in different directions to gather rubbish and add it to the blaze. When all the rubbish was burnt they tidied up around the bonfire raking the remaining embers into a heap so only a pile of ash would be left.

"Now the next thing we could do with is a washing machine to make our lives a bit easier. I'm fed up with washing our clothes in the sink, and soaking things overnight in a bucket," said Sean.

"And when it's your socks Dad, pooh what a smell!"

Tim darted out of the way as his dad made a playful swing to clip him round the ear.

Later that day they headed down into the village. Pulling up at Joe Maxwell's garage Sean got out.

"Anybody at home?"

There was no reply, so he went in the direction of the workshop round the back, spotting Joe down the pit under a car.

"How do Joe."

Joe glanced up.

"Hi Sean, and what can I do for you?"

"Just some diesel."

"Ok, be right with you."

Joe climbed the steps at the far end of the pit. He came outside and the two walked round to the pumps. Removing the filler cap Joe put the nozzle into the pick-up and began filling the tank.

"By the way Sean, I had her ladyship in here last week. You know, her from the big house in the woods."

This woman Joe was referring to wasn't really a lady but the way she acted you'd think she was. She was a tall skinny woman in her sixties. She dressed in the finest clothes though some of the garments showed their age and were going threadbare round the edges. Her eyesight was failing and she squinted all the time. She was never without a feather boa around her neck and the whole outfit was topped off with a wide brimmed hat. She would waltz around the village as though she owned it, followed by her chauffeur, walking her miniature poodle. The chauffeur also cared for the garden, looked after the house and attended to her every need. He had been with her for so long he knew nothing else and had reached that age where he was too old to start afresh.

The lady lived in Bowcock Manor, a large house set in acres of grounds, now mostly overgrown, with nature reclaiming what was hers. The house, once fine, had hosted many big balls, special occasions and garden parties and had been run by an army of servants who had lived in the attic rooms. Gardeners had tended the manicured lawns. This lady had married into money. Her husband had been an industrialist, but she had driven him to drink and an early grave. Her fortune was almost gone and she had no heir to inherit or to take care of her. Rumours were rife around the village that she wanted to sell up.

"Anyway," Joe continued. "While I was filling up her car with petrol last week, she happened to mention that she had a couple of old cars she would like to dispose of, so later that day I went up to take a look. She had an old station wagon, a Ford Prefect and a Sunbeam, all in a pretty poor condition, but they were salvageable, so I made her an offer and she accepted."

"But what has this got to do with me?" Sean interrupted, knowing that once Joe got going he would prattle on for ages.

"I'm coming to that."

Joe paused to extract the pump and replace the filler cap. He leaned against the pick-up.

"So anyway, while I'm up there I take a look around don't I, and I comes across this old caravan in one of the garages."

"What type of caravan?"

Sean's ears pricked up now. Tim was sitting in the pick-up tapping his fingers on the dash board.

"An old traveller's van all complete and in pretty good shape. You interested?"

"Too right! When can I take a look? Sean sounded impatient.

"See me tomorrow, mid morning or thereabouts," replied Joe. Taking the money for the fuel he headed back into his work shop.

Chapter 5. Lady of the Manor

The next day couldn't come quick enough for Sean; he had told
Tim all about his conversation with Joe and now Tim was
excited. The two of them had grown very close in the time they
had lived together on their smallholding; they had no secrets
between each other. Tim acted and behaved a lot older than
his years because he had always been around grownups.

Dead on the dot of ten o'clock they arrived at Joe's, only
to find the place all locked up and deserted. They were left
kicking their heels for almost three quarters of an hour. They
heard the noise of a blown exhaust long before they saw the
vehicle. It was Joe's. Pulling onto his forecourt Joe leaned out
of the van's open window.

"Thought you'd left the country," said Sean.

"Why, what's up, been waiting long? Joe remarked with
surprise.

"Not that you'd notice! So can we get going now?"
Sean's impatience was showing through his raised voice.

"Hop in then, we'll go up in mine."

Joe leaned over to open the passenger door. They
climbed in. Tim sat in the middle while his dad swung the door
shut.

They drove through the country lanes heading for
Bowcock Manor. Within half an hour they were turning into
the drive way. Two tall limestone pillars graced the entrance,
taking the strain of the biggest pair of wrought iron gates Tim
had ever seen, with black paint flaking and the metal being
slowly eroded by rust.

Beneath the tree lined drive of copper beech, the
rhododendron bushes were encroaching from both sides,
slowly covering the wide grass verges. The drive twisted and
turned and they went from the shade of the trees and
shrubbery into the midday sun. As they approached the house
the once pristine lawns were now a mass of dandelions and
seed heads, apart from a small area in front of the house where

a table and two benches had pride of place. There were some fallen trees that hadn't been cleared, casualties of the previous year's storms, their roots ripped from the earth. Joe pulled up by the front door.

"Hang on here a mo."

Joe got out of the vehicle leaving the door ajar, and crossed the drive way, the pea shingle crunching under his every step. Sean and Tim watched him climb the six granite steps to the front door which was flanked by two lion statues, their paws resting on shields which bore the family coat of arms. Joe stretched out his arm, his bony hand and wrist sliding out from beneath the sleeve of his boiler suit. He grasped a large brass lion's head knocker. Raising the head he brought it down twice on the striking plate. The sound seemed to thunder through the house ricocheting off the walls as it travelled down the hallway. Joe turned his back on the door walking back down the steps. Putting his hands in his pockets he ran his shoe through the gravel while he waited. Sean and Tim sat in silence, their eyes fixed on the door.

Joe suddenly spun around. They all heard the door handle turning, and then the door slowly opened with someone giving it a final tug as it rubbed on the threshold. Beams of sunlight entered the house across the black and white floor tiles and crept up the wall.

"Good morning Sir, can I help you?

It was Alistair, the chauffeur.

"Yes we've come to have a look at the caravan out back. Is it OK for us to go round?"

"Ah yes, you are the gent that bought Madam's cars. If you would like to head out back I'll inform Madam you're here."

"Ta mate."

Joe came back to his land rover.

"So, it's still on?

"Yes we can go round and take a look."

Joe proceeded to drive in the direction of the old stables through one of the five archways which made up one side of the cobbled court yard. He pulled up and they all got out.

"This way."

31

Joe pointed to the pair of double doors second from the end. He slipped the sliding bolt, grabbed hold of the handles and, with Sean's help, pulled the doors open. Two doves flew out, having got in through a hole in the slate roof.

There before them stood a large box shape, covered in a tarpaulin. It was around ten feet in length and five feet wide.

"Give me a hand."

Joe picked up one corner of the tarpaulin. All three took hold and pulled together. As they walked backwards, the tarpaulin at first resisted, but with more pressure, gave way and started to slide. They walked out into the daylight and the tarpaulin finally yielded sight of the tail end of a caravan, before sinking to the ground sending up a cloud of dust which had gathered over the years. As the air cleared, the stable revealed an exquisite Reading caravan. These caravans, so-called because they were built in the town of Reading, were becoming rare. This was the best one Sean had seen in many a year. He looked over it with all the expertise of a coach builder. Tim climbed up the steps in-between the shafts to take a peek at the interior. The door was in two halves. He pulled the top door open gazing inside. He saw that everything was still as it was the day the van was parked up. He opened the bottom door by releasing the catch, and entered. The curtains, upholstery and bed covers were all matching red velvet. A fine woven rug on the floor covered with dust showed Tim's footprints as he went further inside.

A black cast iron wood burning stove on the left-hand side still had pans on the top. The chimney flue was broken off, where it went through the roof, probably when they pushed it into the stable Tim thought. An open book lay on the side where the reader had left it. There were two windows, one on each side, engraved with flowers edged by a pattern of leaves. Tim could hear his dad and Joe talking outside so went to investigate. Coming down the steps he found his dad lying on his back underneath the caravan looking up at it and tapping the woodwork with his penknife. Leaning against the large back wheel which was as tall as he was, Tim wrote his name in the dust with the toe of his shoe. His dad crawled out, stood up and brushed himself off.

"Joe, she's almost as sound as the day she was built."

"You want to see inside, it's great, Dad!"

All three entered the caravan, Joe bringing up the rear. Without speaking they began looking and poking around. To Tim, the silence was unbearable.

"Dad, is it all right? Is it sound? Can we have it?" Tim didn't wait for an answer in between questions.

"Hang on, slow down, we don't know how much the old girl wants for it yet, could be too rich for our pockets."

On hearing footsteps, all three poked their heads out of the door to be greeted by Madam herself.

"Good day to you, I see you've found it alright."

She tapped the ash from her cigarette, which was held in a long black holder trimmed with bands of gold.

"Are you interested? I wish to dispose of it as soon as possible. I need the space, and I haven't got all day."

"Could be." Sean replied neutrally, not wanting to show that he would do almost anything to get his hands on it.

"Well come on then, don't waste my time."

The lady couldn't conceal her impatience, as all three of them came down out of the caravan.

"What figure do you have in mind?" said Sean hesitantly.

"Around five hundred pounds, I think that would be in order." She fixed her stare on Sean.

"A bit high Ma'am, been left a long time. Needs a lot of work to put her right. How about two hundred and fifty pounds?"

Tim pulled at his dad's coat, for he knew they had more than enough money back home.

"Oh no," she exclaimed, "far too low."

She shook the cigarette stub from her holder, treading it into the cobbles with annoyance, and turned her stare on Joe, for he had brought this deal to her attention. It was becoming obvious that she was desperate for money.

"Four hundred and seventy five," she said.

"Two hundred and seventy five."

"Four hundred and fifty..."

"Three hundred."

She started to pace up and down, her long flowing dress dragging on the ground, her arms folded across her chest. The pitch in her voice increased.

"Four hundred and twenty five."

Sean looked down at the ground. With one weathered hand he rubbed the back of his neck and, turning, he looked at the caravan then at his son. Tim's eyes were trying to speak to him. Sean returned his gaze, then, he winked.

"Three hundred and twenty five," he said.

"This is absurd!"

With more determined steps, her pacing became laboured, she lit another cigarette. Taking a large inhalation, she blew the smoke out in Sean's direction.

"Four hundred."

They had already saved one hundred pounds from the starting price with Sean's negotiating skills, how much farther could he go?

"Three hundred and fifty, and I don't think I can go much higher, because of all the work that needs doing."

"Three hundred and seventy five pounds and not a penny less, that's my final price." The words seemed to stick in her throat.

"Three hundred and seventy five pounds," agreed Sean without hesitation. He offered his hand to seal the deal, remembering not to spit in his palm.

"Do you have the money?" The lady of the house looked down out his outstretched hand, but made no attempt to offer hers.

"You will have your money this very day, when we come back to collect the caravan, if that's convenient, Ma'am."

"Fine. Don't be later than six, we have guests tonight and I do not wish to be disturbed."

Without uttering another word she turned and walked back towards the house.

"Thought you'd lost it at one point there," said Joe.

"No sweat, she was hungry for the money, and her sort are all the same - all front and nothing to back it up."

"How are we going to get it home Dad?"

Joe took command. "That's the easy bit - back to my place, pick up your motor, you drive home and get the money, I'll get the trailer hitched up, call down and pick you both up, and we'll be back here in no time. How's that sound?"

"Dad now that it's ours, are we going to keep it?"

"You bet, Son, that van is going nowhere but home."

By the time they'd driven home, collected the money, then walked back down the drive, Joe was back with his trailer. Soon they were heading back down the drive of the manor house. Joe reversed the trailer between the archways stopping just short of the stable doors.

"You go and sort out the money, Sean. Tim, you come and help me make a start,"

It was ten to five, they had plenty of time, and anyway there was no way Madam was having guests tonight, it was just her way of keeping up appearances, Joe said.

Sean returned to the old stables from concluding the deal and found that Joe and Tim had by now positioned the ramps, ready. Tim grabbed hold of the hook and pulled the cable from the reel.

"How are we doing?" called Sean.

"Almost there."

Tim hurried into the stable.

"I'm just getting the hook attached. OK, take up the slack!"

Joe wound the handle, the ratchet clicking with every turn. "Sean, you get to the front and steer, and Tim you'd best stand aside."

The cable became taut, there were creaking sounds from the caravan, and for the first time in many years it slowly edged forward. Inch by inch it made its way from the darkness of the stable out into the late afternoon sunshine. The first two wheels touched the ramps and up they went, Joe winding for all he was worth. The trailer sank slowly on its springs as it took the full weight of the caravan. Joe secured his end, and then both he and Sean strapped the caravan securely. Tim slid the ramps under the trailer and locked them in place.

There it sat, and, even if its bright red, blue, yellow and green were now a shade past their full glory, it was the most magnificent caravan you could ever wish to see. There were intricate designs painted all over the exterior, some trimmed with gold.

"She's just beautiful... just beautiful."

Sean was unable to avert his gaze. Memories came flooding back to him from the good old days when caravans like this could be seen on many a road.

Joe brought him back down to earth. "Well are we going to get this caravan home today or are we just going to stand here and stare?"

"All right Joe, let's get her covered up. I don't want everybody knowing what we've got."

All three soon had that sorted out and they made the slow drive home, being careful to avoid low hanging branches.

Once back at Dunroamin Joe took great care reversing his trailer to where Sean was indicating. Offloading was less of a sweat. Sean and Tim had laid out some scaffold boards criss-cross on the ground so the caravan's wheels would not sink in.

Finally they secured the cover to keep out the worst of the weather.

"You must have pulled off the deal of the decade," remarked Joe, "and then there's my bill to settle for today's services."

"Cheap at half the price," joked Sean. "I'm sure we can come to some arrangement."

"I'm sure you can. Anyway we'll talk about that another day, and I'm off home for some tea. See you both later."

Joe headed down the drive waving from the open window of his truck. Tim went down to shut the gate after him. Father and son stayed outside for a while peeking under the tarpaulin and admiring their new possession, before going inside for something to eat. Sean sat talking to his son of the plans he had for doing up the caravan, and once again taking to the road, but there would be a difference this time. This time they would be going together.

"Dad, you're the best."

"And you're the best son a dad could ever wish for," Sean replied, with a slightly watery eye.

Chapter 6. Getting ready for the road

The next day saw great activity. Sean and Tim rigged up a makeshift building over the caravan using old timber, sheets of corrugated iron and even the tarpaulin; to protect it, and them, from the weather, while they restored it. Tim cleared out the inside of the caravan and put all the loose covers and fittings in empty boxes to be stored in one of the old railway carriages. His dad gave him a hand to get the old mattress out and they dragged it down to where the old toilet had been; throwing it onto the pile of ashes ready for burning. It was one thing they would not keep for it had become damp and smelled of mould.

When they broke for some lunch, his dad regaled Tim with more stories of the times when he was very young and travelling around the countryside with his parents working the land while his mother sold lucky heather and wooden pegs door to door.

The remainder of the day they toiled away together, Tim always wanting to learn, but sometimes a bit too eager and rushing at things. His dad had to pull him up short saying: "Do it right the first time, don't rush and mess it up."

It was a lovely evening for they had been blessed with the best of weather, so they had their meal outside. Troosh was rolling around on the grass. Sean got a small fire going with a ring of stones around the outside. Once the flames had died down he rested a large black cast iron frying pan across the stones, with a lump of lard sizzling away. Into it went sausages, sliced potatoes, tomatoes cut in half and a couple of rashers of bacon for good measure. Tim brought out the plates, cutlery, and two slices of bread cut thickly and crowned with a good helping of butter.

"Right let's dish up shall we?"

Sean reached into the pan to divide up their feast. They sat on an old oak log with their plates resting on their knees as they tucked in. Tim rolled up a sausage in his bread. With mouth spread wide he took a bite, butter oozing out and dripping on his plate. Troosh sat staring, his gaze going from one to the other, tongue hanging out of one side of his mouth, salivating, waiting to be able to lick the plates clean.

"This is the life, Son, not much money but boy, we live like kings; the simple life is always the best."

Tim nodded in agreement, finishing off the last of his meal before putting his plate down for Troosh, with a few scraps of bacon left as a treat. It was now getting late and there was a chill in the air. The sun had all but gone and soon the land would become bathed in silver shades as the moon got higher in the sky. They attended to the animals then headed in for a shower and a good night's sleep.

"Tim, are you going to get up?"

It was early the next morning.

"Coming Dad"

He donned his dressing gown and came into the kitchen where he found his dad getting breakfast ready. They both sat down and tucked into their cereal and toast, washed down with a mug of tea.

"Let's sort the animals out and then get stuck into the caravan, what do you think?"

"Great! Let me get washed and dressed, I'll do the washing up and join you outside,"

While Tim got ready, Sean made a start; letting out the animals and sorting their feed. He had milked the goats and by the time Tim joined him outside there was just the pigs left to do.

"Get some straw Tim."

"OK, Dad."

Tim grabbed a bale from the stack. Taking a firm grip of the twine he swung it over his shoulder and, walking up to the pig pen, he threw it over the fence. Cutting the binding he scooped up handfuls of straw and scattered it inside the sty.

"All done, Dad," he called.

"I've done here. Go and let Troosh off so he can have a run around."

Tim did as he was asked.

"What are we doing today?"

"We need to lift the back of the caravan and take off the wheel on the left hand side, because the rim is not tight enough."

"So where do we start?" Tim scratched his head.

"First, we need some blocks, a long length of four by four timber and some wedges."

They gathered up the materials required, then stacked up blocks under the rear axle, and put a second slightly higher pile about two feet away.

"Right Tim, place those wedges into position under the axle while I put this lump of timber through."

Tim put them in place, ready and his dad levered on the timber resting on the second pile of blocks. The caravan started to rise. Tim slid the wedges into position under the axle, and Sean released the pressure and pulled out the timber. The wheel was now free of the ground.

"Now that's how you lift nearly a ton in weight without too much trouble."

Sean rubbed his forearm across his brow.

"Hand me that mallet and we'll get this wheel off."

Tim pulled out the mallet from his dad's tool bag and passed it across. Sean started banging at the wheel hub. After a few thumps the securing pin fell to the ground. Once they undid the locking nut they were able to prise the wheel free of the axle and onto the ground. It stood almost five feet in diameter. They rolled it along to their pick-up. Resting it against the side, Tim let down the tailgate. They eventually loaded the wheel and tied it securely. Tim put Troosh back on his wire and they got in the pick-up and headed for the gate. As usual Tim hopped out and closed the gate before rejoining his dad. They were heading for Nearsham.

Stopping off only at the shop, to treat themselves to an ice cream, they drove straight there, finally turning down a muddy track. They came to a halt outside Nearsham forge. With a bit of grunting they got the wheel unloaded and leaned it up against the side wall of the forge. Sean went inside to speak to the blacksmith. The dimly lit forge had stood on the same spot for years, being handed down from father to son. The walls were covered in grime and the wooden bellows lay silent waiting to ignite the slumbering coals. The cold anvil waited in readiness to tap out a tune.

Tim had time to have a poke around and daydream. He sat down on a large pile of old horseshoes which had been thrown out by the blacksmith over many years. Looking skyward he watched the rooks reweaving their nests after the winter gales, readying themselves for another brood. A sparrow hawk was hovering on the wing: The phantom of death. Tim watched it seeking out its prey. It swooped down behind the hedge soon to reappear clasping a small bird in its claws, only to fly across the fields and out of his view.

"Tim?"

"Here, Dad." Tim jumped down off the pile of horseshoes and joined his dad, who had emerged from the forge. Colin the blacksmith stood in the doorway filling the whole frame, wearing a leather apron and a white tee-shirt pitted with holes from the sparks that flew when he was welding. Saying their goodbyes they set off back home, his dad telling Tim that Colin would drop off the wheel in a day or two with a new rim all as good as new.

On the way back home they called in to see Mick the butcher and pick up some supplies and some belly pork for tea. Back at the caravan the first job was to do some washing. Their laundry had been soaking in the sink. The sun was shining along with a slight breeze. The washing would not take long to dry.

Later that afternoon they set about washing down the outside of the old caravan. Tim climbed up a step ladder onto the roof and with a mop and bucket began cleaning it. His dad, with a sponge and a bucket of soapy water, started washing down the paintwork. They soon washed away years of grime. After a good rinse down with clean water and buffing with some old rags, it looked like a new caravan. Where there was the odd bit of flaking paint they scraped it off, then rubbed it down with a piece of fine sandpaper and primed the bare wood.

"There you go, Son, a grand day's work. Come on, let's go and get cleaned up and out of these wet clothes."

They walked back in, Sean with his arm around Tim's shoulder. After they had washed and changed, they sat down with a fresh mug of tea each, dunking some custard cream biscuits.

"Dad, what colour shall we paint it?"

"Let's keep it as close to the original as possible, with maybe some gold in places to put our own stamp on it. Here let's have a look at some books and see."

Sean got up from the table and took a book from the shelf. He knew which to get by the pictures on the cover. The book, a bit tattered on the corners, was entitled: *Camping and Caravans of a Bygone Age*. Retaking his seat, Sean opened the book.

"Ah, here we are - Reading caravans. You'd best read on."

Tim took the book from his dad and started to read some of the extracts out loud.

"Hey, Dad, it says here, traditionally the caravan and its contents were burnt on the owner's death."

"Yes that's right, Son, that's why there are so few left today and Readings were the Rolls Royce of caravans."

"There are some pictures, look, Dad."

Tim manoeuvred the book round so Sean could take a look.

"Just like ours."

They had most of the paint needed to touch up the caravan, only the gold paint needed buying and clear varnish for the top coat. The following days were spent applying the necessary undercoats and topcoats of paint. Tim, not being too good with the brush, had the job of painting the undercarriage and wheels yellow. By the time he had finished it was hard to tell which had more paint on, Tim or the caravan. When they had done they stood back admiring their work.

"Not bad for a couple of traveller boys, eh?"

"I think we've done a great job, Dad."

"Come on let's get cleaned up and go and treat ourselves, what do you say?"

"You bet."

Tim grabbed a rag soaked in white spirit to get the paint off his arms. The late afternoon sun was still warm as they set off.

"Where are we going, Dad?"

"You'll see. Just sit back and enjoy the ride."

Winding their way round the country lanes they finally arrived at Maude's "Ye Old Tea Shop" Maude was a kindly lady, small in stature and she made the most gorgeous homemade cakes and cream teas. They sat at a round table in the corner and gorged themselves until they were full. It was rather quiet in the shop and Maude came out to join them, wiping some flour from her hands with her apron. She pulled up a chair and sat down. Sean and Maude had known each other for a number of years. He kept her supplied with split logs for her open fire.

"So, Sean, what brings you out this way?"

"A treat, Maude. We have been working flat out renovating a Reading caravan."

"Well, it's certainly nice to see you and young Tim."

She ruffled Tim's hair and Tim blushed and pulled away trying to straighten it.

They both told Maude the story of how they had acquired the caravan and of their plans to travel around together and see more of the countryside. Maude was absorbed in their conversation, her chin in the palm of her hand as she rested her elbow on the table.

"Well, when you come back off your travels make sure you call in and see me won't you? I don't know how much longer I can keep this place running. They're talking of putting a new by-pass in and if that's the case then there will be no passing traffic and no trade for me."

"Maude that will be a shame. Of course we will call in and see you."

Sean rose from his chair. With the bill paid they headed home. They sat outside their caravan enjoying the late evening, and listening to nightingales serenading them.

"That is the perfect end to the perfect day," remarked Sean glancing over at Tim, only to see him with eyes shut, fast asleep.

Colin the blacksmith arrived the next day with the repaired wheel. Unloading it they rolled it over to the caravan.

"I say, what a great wagon, I just had to come over and see it," remarked Colin eyeing it up and down.

"Ay, we've put a lot of work into it," replied Sean.

"You want a hand to refit the wheel while I'm here?"

"Cheers Colin."

Sean picked up the mallet. Colin lifted the wheel up and slid it onto the axle with little apparent effort. The locking nut wound on the pin was knocked home and the hub replaced.

"Tim, you ready to take the wedges out?"

"OK."

Tim crouched down underneath.

Sean slid the timber in place; both men grabbed hold of it and pulled down. With Colin's extra muscle it was much easier. Tim pulled the wedges out and the two men slowly let the caravan down.

"Right, Tim; there's a job for you; prepare and paint that wheel. I'll go and settle up with Colin."

The two of them walked off as Tim set about his task, rubbing down and painting. He had read about the design of these caravans. The enormous rear wheels of the Reading caravan had to be set on the outside. The front wheels, being smaller in diameter, fitted underneath, allowing for easier turning in tight places. The caravans were set high because many years ago the country tracks, were rough and developed deep ruts.

By the end of the following week, Sean and Tim had done all the outside work and used gold paint on the scroll work and in fine lines on the spokes of the wheels and down the shafts. The shutters to the windows were taken off and Sean tightened up the joints before fitting new hinges and replacing them.

The next task was re-fitting the inside. Tim had already cleaned out all of the loose fittings so it was ready for a good wash down. It made an incredible difference. The glass panes of the display cabinet and the cut glass mirrors sparkled, and so did the oil lamp which hung on the right hand side, on an angel bracket. This had a vent above it which allowed the fumes to escape but did not let the rain in. The woodwork inside was stained in light and dark oak with sprays of flowers hand painted on the cupboard doors. No new painting was required inside which was a relief to Tim after all the hard work he had put in on the outside. He sat up on the main bunk, which would be his dad's, looking around at what would very soon become their new home. The gypsy caravan could be described as a one room living area on wheels. Beneath where Tim was sitting, there was a moveable shelf which, when pulled out, would form another bunk, where he would sleep.

Tim jumped down off the bunk and walked out of the narrow shuttered door onto the small veranda. There were two seats, one either side, for use when out on the road. Hanging from each corner of the roof were woven ropes with large knotted ends. The steps went into position in-between the shafts and, when not in use, were stored at the rear of the caravan on hooks. Underneath the caravan was a large box, to store pots pans and some food stuffs, always in the shade to keep it cool. There were other hooks where a variety of things could be hung, like buckets, a hay bag for the horse and a small chicken coop to house the bantams.

"Tim, give me a hand will you?" Sean was calling from one of the railway carriages where he was struggling to remove a queenie stove. "Hold this while I pull it out."

Tim ran over and took hold of some sheets of hardboard to stop them falling, and with both hands now free, Sean carried the stove outside. Tim let go of the hardboard and followed. They took the stove to pieces and wire brushed them down, and then black leaded each piece. Two hours later it was dry, buffed up and put back together. Lifting it into the caravan they placed it into position on a small red tiled hearth with the metal back plate already polished. They slotted a new smoke stack into place as the old one was beyond repair.

"We'll use our sleeping bags instead of other bedding, it will make it easier and less to stow away."

"Fine by me, anything for an easy life," said Tim.

"Good that's settled then," said Sean. "And we can use our spare set of curtains in here. You have the two bottom drawers and I'll have these on this side for my clothes."

"Can we start packing now?"

"Bit soon, Son, we've still got a job to do yet."

"What's that Dad?" Tim had disappointment in his voice.

"We need to put some waterproofing on the roof. The green canvas seems in good condition but just in case, and as you are the lighter of the two of us you get the job."

"Thanks Dad, you're a real pal," said Tim with a sullen voice, feeling he had drawn the short straw again. But as it happened it was not too bad. The waterproofing solution was a clear liquid, very watery and went on easily, drying to a transparent finish and totally waterproof.

Tim climbed down. "All finished, Dad, are we ready now?"

"Well, there's one last thing."

"But Dad, surely there can't be anything else left to do?"

"Who's going to pull the caravan?"

Chapter 7. Appleby Fair

A few days later, straight after breakfast Sean had a surprise for Tim.

Pack a bag Tim; we're going for an overnight stay."

"Where will we be staying?"

"We're taking Uncle Jim's horse box and we'll put some fresh straw in the back so we can sleep in there, so don't forget our sleeping bags."

Rolling up the sleeping bags Tim tied them with twine then put a change of clothes each into a holdall for himself and his dad.

"I'm ready, Dad."

Sean was coming in from sorting out the animals. At that moment, the horse box pulled up outside and then Jim came into the caravan.

"Brewing tea?"

"Kettle's already boiled, help yourself," called Sean, now in the bedroom where he was hastily throwing the quilt over his bed and tidying up. Jim made tea and sat down at the table. Sean came through.

"How do Jim, how's missus?"

"Fine, you know, as always. So, is young Tim all excited about going away?"

"You bet. He's running about like a headless chicken."

Jim gulped his tea down and smiled.

"I'd best be making tracks, you best had too."

They all emerged from the caravan and Sean locked it and gave Jim the keys. They unhitched the horse box from Jim's motor and secured it onto their pick-up.

"Don't worry about anything;" said Jim, "I'll look after the place while you're gone."

"Thanks, Mate. I owe you one."

And with that, Sean and Tim drove away.

They were heading for the small market town of Appleby; a journey of about three and half hours, and as they got nearer to their destination they passed more and more traditional traveller caravans on the road. These were lighter types of vehicle, with canvas tops, like the Openlot, and the Bowtop which were more common in the north of England.

It was Tuesday in the second week of June, a glorious day and not a cloud in the sky. As they came into Appleby, people were milling everywhere. Heading for Gallows Hill they parked alongside the cars, vans pick-ups and horse boxes of all types. Among the mass of vehicles, small caravans were staking claim to their patches of grass. It was the first time that Tim had been to Appleby. He stared around taking in all the sights and sounds, while his dad told him of the early days when he used to come here with Uncle Jim.

Sean spoke of when he was a small boy, when horses and caravans would line all the roads for many miles around for days before the start of the fair. It was a place for families and friends to meet up, often the only meeting they would have all year. They would exchange tales and catch up on all the gossip.

"The Appleby horse fair," Sean said proudly, "is the largest gathering of travelling and gypsy people in Britain."

They walked down into the village itself where hordes of people stood outside the public houses, glasses in hand, all raising their voices trying to be heard.

Everybody was in very high spirits and enjoying one another's company.

"Dad I'm hungry." Tim rubbed his stomach.

"OK, let's see what we can find."

Sean looked over the sea of heads in front of him.

"Over there: fish and chips; will that do?"

"Smashing," replied Tim "I'm famished."

Crossing the road, they joined the end of the queue and not too long after, they found themselves at the counter.

"Two large fish and chips and mushy peas, please."

"Salt and vinegar sir?"

"Yes please."

Wrapping their meals up in newspaper, the lady handed the parcels across, taking their money and giving back their change.

"Next!" She shouted.

They worked their way back out of the crowd and found a spot on the green to sit down. Sean handed Tim his parcel, the newspaper stained with grease from cooking. Unwrapping the food on their laps they both tucked in, to fish fresh from Whitby in a rich golden-brown batter, and chips done to perfection. When he bit into the battered ball of mushy peas, Tim found a cloud of steam released, and he sucked in mouthfuls of fresh air trying to cool it down. Finishing their meal, they licked their fingers, screwed up the paper and dropped it in the bin.

"What's next, Dad?"

"Let's take a look at the horse trading."

They wandered down to the main street where owners were running their ponies and horses up and down at a furious pace, trying to impress prospective buyers. They stood for a while watching the comings and goings.

"Hello Sean, long time no see."

A voice came from behind, followed by a friendly slap on the back. "See you've got your boy with you then."

Sean turned round and saw his old pal, Stick. The name came from his appearance. He was tall and skinny. You'd probably see more meat on a butcher's pencil.

"Hi, Stick, what brings you up here?"

"Doing some business with me horses. Why, you looking for one?"

"I could be. Have you run yours yet?"

"No, I'll leave mine till tomorrow. Do you fancy taking a look at them?"

They weaved their way out of the thronging crowd and headed for the outskirts of the village, back to Gallows Hill, with Stick leading the way. They strode over to the far side where there were six horses tethered to a makeshift rail. As they approached Stick's caravan, his wife popped her head out of the open door.

"Mary, look who I've found," he said to her.

Sean and Mary exchanged pleasantries. The men then walked over to have a look at the horses. One animal immediately took Sean's eye but he went over to one of the others instead, rubbing his hand along its back and down its rear right leg lifting the hoof to inspect it. In the background he could hear that Stick was giving him earache babbling on about each horse's history. But Sean knew Stick from old; he had probably not long bought these horses himself and didn't have a clue where they came from. But he let him carry on, and finally he reached the horse that he was interested in. He gave it close inspection; looking in its mouth to see the state of its teeth to make out its age. The horse was a well built beast, a Shire cross, standing near fourteen hands high, black and white in colour. Now the haggling started.

"That one's worth four and a half hundred of any body's money." Said Stick.

"You jest. I could buy one of the Queen's horses for that, and have some change."

"Four then."

"No, two."

"Don't waste my time, I won't even get my money back at that price and, I can tell you for a fact, that horse has been harnessed up and trained to pull a wagon, and got a good temperament."

"Not my fault you paid too much for that horse."

The to-ing and fro-ing went on for another ten minutes. Sean had already decided how much he was prepared to pay. At last, the two men came to an agreement, three hundred and twenty pounds. They slapped hands on the deal. Sean reached into his pocket pulled out a wad of notes and settled his debt.

Sean and Tim were now proud owners of a fine horse. Stick slipped on a halter rope and released the tether.

"All yours now Sean, you strike a hard bargain."

"Don't give me that, Stick, you still did alright."

"Ay, maybe not too bad."

"We'll be seeing you."

Sean gave Tim the halter rope and off they went, making their way back to their pick-up. Reaching the spot where they had parked, Sean opened the side door to the trailer, and then hung the full hay bag which they had brought with them on the outside. Leading the horse Tim tied it up next to the hay. Sean closed the side door.

With the horse secure, off they went again. This time they went down to Sandside by the river bridge, as this was the spot where the travellers washed their horses. They rested a while watching horses of all sizes being given a good scrub down. Then they wandered towards where the salesmen could be found. Here, travelling people could buy anything and get any service they required. Waterford Crystal and Royal Crown Derby were very popular, and there were knick knacks of all sorts and even fortune tellers.

They stopped at the harness maker with all his wares displayed, hung on racks and spread on the ground. Sean sorted out what they needed and paid for it. Then; slinging the leather ware over his shoulder they carried on down the rows of stalls past pottery, jewellers, and brush and peg makers.

"Afternoon, Sean."

Sean glanced over in the direction of the familiar voice. It was Colin, the blacksmith. He was shoeing a large black mare.

"How's it going, have you finished that wagon yet?" Colin enquired.

"All done, just needs us to pack our stuff up. How's business?"

"Not too bad, no complaints." Colin picked up the horse's left rear leg and clamped it between his knees.

"I'm glad I bumped into you," said Sean, "we've bought a Shire cross and it could do with re-shoeing ready for the road. So if you're available, could you come by, once we're home?"

"Fine I'll be round tomorrow on my way back."

And Colin disappeared in a cloud of smoke, as he placed a red hot shoe on the horse's hoof.

Tim as ever was thinking of food.

"Dad I'm hungry can we get something to eat?"

"Sure, what do you fancy?"

Tim led his dad over to the burger van and they bought a couple of cheeseburgers and a can of drink each. Time was getting on. The traders had started to pack away their wares before the night's festivities started.

Sean and Tim returned to their pick-up and made sure their new horse was fed and watered before they tucked into their burgers. Then they rolled out their sleeping bags on the thick bed of straw. They brushed their teeth rinsing out their mouths with their last drops of fizzy drink. With the horse tied up outside they settled down inside the trailer for the night.

Next morning Tim was awake and dressed before his dad. He stuffed a chamois leather in his back pocket. The he untied the horse and took it down to Sandside. He led the docile beast into the river. The horse seemed to love the water going in without hesitation. Tim gave him a good wash with the leather.

When he got back to where they had parked he found his dad awake, resting on his elbows, looking out of the back of the trailer and squinting into the early morning sunlight.

"Morning Son, good night's kip?"

"Fine, Dad. You?"

"Slept like a log."

"I took the horse down for a bath, he loved it."

Sean climbed out of the trailer, and had a good stretch.

"Well done, Son! I reckon we'd best be making tracks."

They rolled up their bedding, put the harness, and other equipment they had bought, into the back of the pick-up, and then led the horse into the trailer and fastened the ramp. They were off, heading for home, only stopping off at a transport cafe for breakfast.

They made good time, arriving home just after lunch. Troosh was overjoyed to see them, barking and standing on his hind legs straining at his lead. Unloading the horse, Tim led him across to one of the paddocks and opened the gate. He beckoned him in. Releasing him he watched the horse gallop around. His dad joined him and they sat on the top rail of the five bar gate.

"We have to think of a name for him, we can't keep calling him 'horse'."

Pondering for a moment Tim said, "Chalky."

"OK, Chalky it is."

The tooting of a horn sounded. "That will be Colin; you'd best go let him in."

Tim jumped down and ran to open the gate at the bottom of the drive.

"Where is this new horse then?"

"Down the back, Dad's there."

"Fine looking beast Sean," said Colin, climbing out of his truck. "Did you get him at a good price?"

"Stick made me pay the going rate."

Colin connected up the gas bottle to his portable furnace and fired it up. It roared into life and the heat could be felt six feet away. Tim had Chalky on his halter and now he led him out of the paddock and tied him to the side of the pick-up.

"I see your boy's got a natural way with horses."

"Ay that he has," remarked Sean with pride.

Colin set to with the task in hand. Smoke billowed and the air rang with the sound of the hammering in of nails. Soon the job was done.

"There you go, they will last you on your travels. When are you off?"

"Next couple of days, all being well," said Tim smiling.

Colin collected up his tools and having been paid for his time he bid his farewells, wishing them a safe trip.

Tim and his dad decided to try Chalky with the caravan to see how he would cope. Retrieving the new harness from the back of the pick-up they got him ready. Tim held on to Chalky's halter as his dad raised the shafts. Slowly, Tim encouraged the horse to walk backwards. Once he was in position Sean clipped him on, adjusting the straps where necessary. Then, threading the reins through the hoops, he climbed aboard the caravan. Taking up the slack, he got Tim to remove the chocks from underneath the wheels. Then with Tim once again holding Chalky's bridle, Sean gave him the command and Chalky leaned into his harness taking the weight of the caravan. The leather tightened, the shafts lifted slightly and with a creak, the caravan started to move forward.

"Come ahead, Chalky, come on." Said Tim.

The caravan edged out of their makeshift shelter.

"Walk him around the yard a few times Tim."

Four times round they went and then Tim let go of the bridle. His dad took over on the reins, pulling to the left and then to the right. Chalky took to it like a duck to water, his tail swishing and head held high. The tricky job of reversing back into the shelter went without a hitch. Putting the chocks back in place, Tim released Chalky and undressing him of his harness, he took him back to the paddock. Sean told Tim that they would take to the road the next day for a trial run. Tim was restless all night; all he could think about was tomorrow for it could not come quick enough.

After breakfast when the chores were completed, they got Chalky ready and hooking him up they were ready for the off. Tim climbed aboard with his dad.

"It's no good looking at me; if you don't take the reins we won't be going anywhere," said Sean.

A big grin came across Tim's face as he reached forward to grab hold of the reins.

"Move on!"

With a slight crack of the reins on his back Chalky moved on, pulling them out of the shed. They went round to the left and headed for the gate. Sean jumped down to open the gate, Tim drove through slowly. His dad closed the gate and climbed aboard.

"This is fantastic, Dad."

"Ay, not bad is it? You just concentrate on the road."

As they rolled gently along the quiet country lanes people turned to look at them. The sound of Chalky's new shoes on the tarmac road accompanied them. There were even people stopping to take photos. They were heading for Joe Maxwell's garage. Chalky was taking it all in his stride while Tim was in his element, handling the caravan with ease.

"Pull up here, Son," called Sean as they reached Joe's place. Tim pulled on the brake and tied the reins off. They both jumped down. Joe was in the front shop, sorting out a delivery of parts that had just arrived. Sean tapped on the window. Looking up Joe smiled and headed for the door then he stopped in his tracks.

"What a wagon, never in my life have I seen a more splendid one, all that hard work has paid off. By Jove I wish I was coming with you!"

"Pack a bag and come," said Tim.

"Wish I could lad, but unfortunately I'm needed here. I've got no one else to take over. Maybe another time. Hang on; I've got something for you.

Joe disappeared back into the shop. He was right about the caravan. As Chalky stood there on the forecourt with the caravan in tow, it looked great with all the bright colours gleaming in the sunshine. Even the windows had a sparkle. Joe returned with a camera.

"Take this. Here's a couple of extra films. You can take some pictures and show them to me when you get back, OK?"

Tim's face lit up.

"Thanks Joe, I'll do that and I'll take good care of your camera."

"You keep it, Lad. It's no use to me now, anyway I must get on. Be safe on your travels." Joe stepped back.

Releasing the brake, Sean and Tim set off waving goodbye. They took the long way home not saying much to each other, just taking in the sheer delight of their surroundings. That night they filled the caravan with everything they needed and packed all their clothes. Tomorrow was the big day. Sean had arranged for Jim to come and keep an eye on the place and care for the animals while they were gone. Troosh would be going with them.

Chapter 8. Their adventures begin with a sting in the tail

It was a misty start to the day with some light drizzle in the air but that didn't dampen their spirits. Jim and Sonny had arrived to see them off. After they had all eaten a hearty breakfast together, they said their goodbyes. Tim and his dad hitched up Chalky to the caravan and, with Troosh trotting alongside they set out for a new adventure in life together.

"I never dreamed this would ever happen to us, Dad."

"Well, Son, you'd best pinch yourself. It's happening so sit back and enjoy it."

They ambled along pulling in every now and then to let the traffic that had built up behind them, go past. Mid afternoon they decided to leave the road and set up camp for the night.

"That will do for the first day; we don't want to tire out Chalky too much."

Sean pulled on the reins to bring the horse to a halt, telling his son to chock up the wheels. They unhitched Chalky and staked him out on the wide verge, allowing him to crop the grass and rest.

"Best look for some firewood, Tim, if we are going to have anything to eat tonight."

"Ok Dad."

Tim wandered off along the hedgerow in search of some suitable sticks. Returning after some twenty minutes he was laden with a huge bundle of dried wood. He dropped it down by the ring of stones his dad had made ready. Collecting some dried grass and placing this in the middle, Tim laid small twigs over for kindling, then struck a match and set the dried grass alight. Once it was blazing, his dad seized branches from the bundle Tim had brought and broke them over his knee. Placing these on top they soon had a roaring fire. They carried a couple of water containers on the van just in case there was no water where they stopped. Tim went round the back to unhook the cage that housed the bantams and, placing this on the ground, he let them out. Ruffling their feathers the bantams stretched and began pecking up the corn that Tim had scattered on the ground. Reaching into their cage Tim retrieved two eggs from the straw.

His dad had banged the hook-iron into the ground and set the kettle over the fire. Their frying pan was resting across the stones to one side, warming. It had a long handle so you could pick it up without burning yourself. Into the frying pan went rashers of bacon and sausages. Tim put the eggs on the grass as they would be the last to go in. Two chunks of bread went into the pan, for fried bread.

"A feast fit for a king. Go and get the plates, Tim."

Tim had beaten his dad to it, for even as Sean spoke he was coming out of the caravan with the plates. The blue smoke slowly rising from the fire was mixed with the noise of sizzling sausages and the smell lingered in the air getting their taste buds going. Troosh lay on the porch of their caravan with his head between his paws, drooling.

Sean delved into the frying pan to serve up their meal and they both tucked in with haste, enjoying every mouthful. Tim felt that this was the perfect life, living off the land and sleeping under the stars. It was fantastic. They both left some scraps for Troosh. After the chores his dad made two mugs of tea. Tim got out an old tattered map of Britain which he had bought from a jumble sale some time before. They began discussing the route they would take the next day while Sean poured some hot water into a bowl and set about having a shave.

"We'll pick up some work on the way," he said. "We do have some money but it won't last forever, and anyway, work is all part of being on the road."

"What sort of work, Dad?"

"Well we should be able to get some potato picking or fruit picking, and a bit of wheeling and dealing - anything that makes us a few bob."

"I'm up for that."

They sat talking until the moon was up and it turned a bit chilly. The fire had died right down and there were just some glowing embers.

"Best make a move, Tim, getting near bedtime."

They rose to their feet and Sean put the last of the wood on the fire, to keep it going until morning. Tim went and gathered up the bantams and put them in their cage to keep them safe from the fox. They climbed up into the caravan and pulling out the sleeping shelf for Tim they unrolled their sleeping bags.

"Did you know, Tim, that in winter, travellers used to get some of the stones from around the fire, wrap them up in cloth, and put them in their beds for warmth?"

"The travellers' answer to electric blankets!"

"Yes you could say that, Son, I'll just check on Chalky."

Sean climbed down from the caravan and went over to where the horse was tethered. Leaning down he checked the peg was secure in the ground and, patting the horse on the neck he returned. Troosh lay underneath the van, grass flattened. He was settled for the night. All was quiet. Breaking the stillness came from the hooting of an owl close by. Far off in the distance a church clock struck the hour. The sound pierced the still air. There was the odd crackle from the fire. Soon they had both drifted off into a deep sleep.

The dawn chorus woke them. Tim turned over and buried his head inside his sleeping bag. Sean got up, stepping over his son and opened the doors. He sat on the top step watching the sun rise above the tree line, drinking in the scenery. Climbing down he went over to the fire with its ashes still smouldering. Raking the white ashes to one side with a stick he gave a gentle blow and the exposed charcoal reignited. Topping up the kettle he placed it on the hook-iron then went to let out the bantams. Next he checked the horse, and then placed the frying pan over the burning embers to soften up the fat from last night. He threw in six rashers of bacon.

"Tim," he called out. "Are you getting up or do I give your bacon butties to Troosh?"

Tim stirred into life, stretching his arms above his head. The smell of his dad's cooking wafted into the caravan and it was too much to resist. Kicking off his sleeping bag he pulled on his jeans. Barefoot, he went outside, rubbing his eyes in the now bright sunlight, and he could see Chalky munching away on the dew laden grass, quite content. By about ten o'clock they were ready for the off, everything stowed away. The only evidence that they had stayed there was a small round burnt patch of grass.

"Oh I almost forgot," said his dad as he disappeared into the caravan leaving Tim holding the reins. Tim could hear his dad rummaging about in one of the drawers.

"There you go." Sean handed his son a bag.

"What is it?"

"Open it and see."

Tim passed the reins over to his dad, and opened the bag. Putting his hand inside, he pulled out a new flat cap and a red neckerchief.

"Thanks, Dad!"

"Well I thought you'd best look the part."

So they sat there, father and son, in flat caps and scarves with Chalky ambling along at a leisurely pace. Once again his dad regaled Tim with stories of his past days on the road and all the different jobs he had done, and the places he had visited during the time that Tim had stayed with his aunties. Tim was fascinated, wanting to know every detail.

Suddenly there was a loud honking and a screech of tyres. A big estate car roared past, swaying all over the road, the driver with his arm out of the window shaking his fist. Chalky faltered slightly but continued his stride.

"Blasted road hogs!" Sean stood up on the porch returning the gesture followed by two fingers. "Why have people got to be in such a rush these days? Henry Ford has a lot to answer for." He sat back down.

Tim smiled as he looked at his dad who continued to mutter to himself. The remainder of their travels that day passed without further incident.

"This looks a good spot, how about stopping here for a while, Son?"

They were close by an inn.

"Handy for the pub, Dad."

Both chuckling they got down. Tim blocked up the wheels, taking stock of the Fox and Hounds public house. It was an old barn conversion. Sean got Chalky's feed bag from the back, put some oats in it and strapped it to his bridle. By this time a few people had gathered outside the pub. A caravan of such splendour on the road was a rarity. Sean and Tim wandered over to the pub.

"Hang on here, Son while I pop inside."

Tim sat on one of the seats outside the pub. It had been cut from an old forty-five gallon oak barrel. Other upturned barrels were used for tables. With arms folded and leaning back he listened to the other people paying compliments and saying how smart their rig looked.

"There you go, Son."

His dad came out of the pub holding a tray which he placed on the table. There were two pints: beer for him and shandy for Tim. There were two thick slices of homemade pork pie with egg in the middle and two packets of crisps. Tim grabbed his slice of pork pie with both hands and started to devour it.

"Don't get too close to that horse!"

Sean called a warning to one of the strangers admiring the rig. Troosh lay down in the doorway of the caravan his eyes following every move the strangers made.

"While I was getting our drinks I was chatting to the landlord about any work that might be going in the area."

"And was there any?" Tim wiped his mouth with the back of his hand.

"Well kind of. He wants to know if we would be interested in cleaning up the pub garden so people could use it again."

"Sounds fine to me."

"Right that settles it. I'll tell him we'll do it. He's offered to feed us and a few bob on top."

Sean got up from the table and went back inside the pub. It made Tim feel good that his dad had asked him before taking the job. His dad came back out, rolling up the sleeves of his shirt.

"Deal done. We can pull the caravan up round the back, and the landlord said the farmer won't mind us letting Chalky out in the field there."

Tim returned to the caravan and drove it round the back. When it was safely parked up, Sean unhitched Chalky and led him into the field. There was no need to stake the horse as the field was well hedged and secured with a five bar gate. Tim walked over and collected some small logs from the wood pile leaning up against one of the outhouses. There was also an outside toilet they could use. Tim thought to himself it was better than taking a shovel and digging a hole behind a bush which is what they were doing out on the road. Going back into the caravan with the wood, he proceeded to get the queenie stove going ready for a brew. Sean returned once he was sure Chalky had settled. He let the bantams out.

"Everything OK, Tim?"

"Fine Dad, stove's on the go. Where do we get the water from?"

"There should be an outside tap over by the back door, the landlord said."

Tim headed off in that direction and it was just where his dad had said, underneath the scullery window by the back door. The concrete under the tap was wet and there was green mould growing up the wall where the tap had long been leaking. He started to fill the kettle and just then the door opened.

"Hi kid, here, the wife told me to give you this."

Tim turned off the tap and put the kettle on the ground and the landlord handed over a large bowl which contained sausages, home cured ham, four pieces of pork pie, some black pudding, two eggs, a lump of cheese and two wedges of fruit cake balanced on the top.

"That should keep you going, and here's something for your dog."

It was a big knuckle bone and it still had a fair bit of meat on it.

"Thank you, Sir."

Tim, caught up the kettle and, cradling the bowl in his arms, headed back to the caravan. With arms laden and the kettle swinging, he struggled up the steps.

"Give us a hand, Dad."

His dad came to his aid and grabbed the bowl.

"Where have you been, Son, raiding the larder?"

"No, the landlord's wife sorted it out for us."

"This job could take us a lot longer than we first thought, eh!" Sean joked, tucking into a piece of pork pie and winking.

They cooked the bacon and sausages and with the frying pan cooling beside the stove, they devoured their meal with zest. Sitting back, unable to eat another mouthful Tim rubbed his stomach. Troosh was underneath the van his front legs wrestling to grip the bone. Sean poured out their second cup of tea.

"Right, who's washing up?"

"You wash, I'll dry, Dad."

"Come on then."

His dad collected the plates and cups, placing them in the bowl and pouring in hot water. The two of them set to work and soon had everything all clean and tidy. Boiling more water they both had a wash then hit their bunks for a good night's sleep.

Soon it was eight o'clock in the morning and they were woken by the sound of rattling bottles. It was the landlord sorting out the empties from the night before. Sean poked his head out of the door.

"Morning, Gove'nor."

"Morning, Sean. Fine day. Wife's cooking a spot of breakfast. It'll be ready in about twenty minutes, OK?"

"Great," replied Sean as he struggled to put his shirt on. Reaching out with his foot he gave Tim a kick.

"What's up?" said Tim in a stupor.

"Come on, rise and shine, breakfast is almost ready."

Sean poured cold water into the bowl to have a quick wash. He flicked some water into Tim's face.

"Come on, move yourself."

Tim got up, washed and dressed and, as they came down the steps, they heard the call of: "Breakfast!"

Heading for the open back door, Tim ran his fingers through his hair to tidy it up. They entered the kitchen and the landlord's wife beckoned them to take a seat. The landlord was already seated with his head buried in the morning's newspaper. After they had all finished their breakfast the landlord rose to his feet. Pushing his chair back he grabbed a bunch of keys from the sideboard.

"Come on then, best get started."

Leading the way he showed them where all the tools were kept.

"There you go; you should find all you need. If not just shout."

Then he turned and headed back to the pub.

Sean ventured inside the shed and, putting some tools into the wheelbarrow, steered it out of the door. They walked over to the play area and garden. On reaching it, Tim stood in the middle of what had once been a nice lawn but was now knee high grass and weeds. The plants around the outside had become overgrown and entangled.

"Some job we've got here Dad." Tim looked glumly around.

"It's not that bad, once we get stuck in you will see a difference."

His dad was trying to be positive. He started to unload the tools.

"I'll cut the grass while you come behind me with the rake."

Sean was an expert with a scythe. He swung his body from the waist and the scythe went from side to side, skimming the ground with great precision. The cut grass fell in neat layers all ready for Tim to collect and put in the wheelbarrow. Every now and then Sean would pause, stand the scythe up on its handle, and taking out a rounded sharpening stone from his back pocket, proceed to run it along the full length of the blade, checking the sharpness with his thumb. Then it was back to work, the blade slicing through the rough grass like a hot knife through butter. They stopped briefly and had a ploughman's lunch of pickles, bread and cheese washed down with a fizzy drink.

*

Three days later and the job was complete; grass cut, borders reinstated with crisp clean edges, roses and shrubs pruned, and Sean even had time to put up some hanging baskets. The landlord and his wife were very pleased with the result and customers were already enjoying the garden.

In their time at the pub Sean and Tim lived very well. Their greatest luxury was to be able to do all their washing regularly, (though as they had no iron they put the next day's shirt under their sleeping bag while they slept, so it would be pressed in the morning).

The day they left, the landlady gave them some more pie, cheese and pickles, along with meat and potatoes, bread and some home grown tomatoes. Tim helped himself to some small logs for their queenie stove, and they topped up their water containers. The landlord settled up with Sean, and they headed off, promising to call in the next time they passed by.

Back on the open road and heading for greener pastures, they made for Lower Pinewood farm because, Sean told Tim, he had called there some years back with Jim, while working the rounds potato picking.

"We've got tea for tonight at any rate; I shall enjoy those chops the landlady gave us with some fried potatoes."

"I can taste them already Dad." Tim licked his lips.

At about mid morning they turned off the road and went down an enticing track. There were overhanging trees on either side. It was carpeted with lush green grass verges. The sun glistened through the branches causing dappled shade. Chalky ambled along and Tim and his dad lay back, soaking up the sun's rays. Troosh had jumped down and was ahead by two hundred yards, every now and again looking over his shoulder checking his companions were following. A long low ash branch hung across the track laden down with the season's seed heads. As they passed, the branch bent forward then brushed along the side of the caravan. Finally free, the branch swung back with a whack. Tim and his dad looked at each other on hearing the odd sound, but thinking no more of it they rested back, delighting in the heat from the sun. A buzzing sound got louder and louder, and then a dark shadow loomed.

Unbeknown to them, when the branch swung back, the sound they heard was it hitting a bee's nest! Now they were inundated. Chalky's ears pricked up and he became agitated, shaking his head and snorting. Some of the angry bees were landing on him with their abdomens pushing through his thick coat ensuring their stings hit the mark. More and more came and both Tim and his dad swatted them but to no avail. Chalky reared up and went into a trot, then a canter and finally a full gallop. Tim reached up and clung onto the rope hanging from the porch roof.

His dad fell backwards through the open door still holding on to the reins. The caravan was now in full flight, careering down the track at top speed with pots and pans crashing about inside. Troosh was running hell for leather to maintain his lead. The caravan hit a rut and Tim took to the air clinging on for dear life, now outside the caravan with his gangly legs swinging as if he was running in mid air. Sean was pulling with all his might, hollering at the top of his voice, but Chalky had other ideas.

A glistening could be seen ahead. As they got nearer Sean could make out that it was a stream, and his eyes widened. The reins were so tight around his hands that they cut off the blood and his hands went white. Through the stream they went and water sprayed up both sides. Sean got Chalky under control at last; slowing down to a canter and then coming to a stop. The horse was exhausted and so hot, steam was coming off his whole body and he was still shaking his head and swishing his tail. Sean jumped down to soothe him and, taking the bridle, he guided the horse to a patch of grass in a clearing among the trees to one side of the track.

"Dad, Dad!" Tim now with his feet back on the porch pulled on the brake.

"OK, Son, come on down. Let's get Chalky out of his harness and settle him."

They undid the hooks and straps and led Chalky out from the shafts, walking him back to the stream. They stood in the water splashing it over Chalky trying to cool him down. No bees had followed and the air was still. Leading the horse back they pegged him out. Chalky sank to his knees then rolled over to scratch the annoying stings.

Tim and his dad then attended to themselves. Lumps and bumps had appeared on all of their exposed skin.

"Best get some cream on these stings, Lad."

"OK, Dad, it's in the bottom drawer."

But as they turned to look through the open doorway, a dismaying sight greeted them. All the drawers were open and all their things were scattered on the floor topped off with their sleeping bags.

"It's where, Son?"

"Um...er...well it's in there somewhere!"

This raised a smile and then laughter from both of them, such was their relief that they were both unharmed.

"The bantams, Dad!" exclaimed Tim.

Running round the rear, he unhitched their cage. Laying it down on the grass he released the clasp. Three very shaken and dazed bantams emerged, ruffling their feathers and stumbling about as though they were tipsy.

That evening was spent tidying and replacing their belongings back in the drawers. They were unable to find the cream. All they had was Chalky's liniment for soothing aches and sprains so they rubbed that over their stings. There were no eggs as the birds had broken them when the caravan careered down the track. So for tea they just settled for bread and cheese with squashed tomatoes washed down with a brew of black tea. They spent the night under the stars in the open air as the liniment stank so much. Troosh slept in the caravan curled up on Tim's bunk as he could not stand the smell either.

Chapter 9. Picture perfect

The next morning when they woke, the smell of the liniment had gone and Chalky, none the worse for his experience, was munching the dew-laden grass. The bantams were still a bit twitchy. Tim was first to rise and he was having a good stretch when his dad threw back the covers and joined him. Tim threw a towel over his shoulder and they went to the stream for a morning wash. Stripping down to their underwear they edged their way into the middle of the chilly water, and, taking scoops of water in their hands, they washed themselves down. Gingerly making their way back over the stony riverbed, they picked up their clothes and hurried back to the caravan. After rubbing themselves down they put on fresh clothes. It was a lazy start to their day. Having packed everything up, they trundled on at a slow pace with Sean walking alongside Chalky, holding his bridle.

Just after lunch, they pulled into a small village. Securing the caravan they entered the local store to top up their provisions. Once these were stowed away, they made their way on for a few more miles. It was gone five when they decided to make camp. Rather than light a fire outside that night, Tim got the queenie stove going. Soon the caravan was filled with the smell of sizzling pork chops and sliced potatoes. Sean had laid out their plates and dishes, for tonight they were having tinned peaches for pudding. Sitting on the porch they tucked into their meal, while Troosh made short shrift of the bones.

"We should be at the farm by nightfall tomorrow if all goes well. We might even meet up with some of the other travellers."

"Bet none of them have a caravan like ours, Dad," said Tim with pride.

"Grab your torch, Son, let's go and see what we can find."

There was a chill in the air so they put on their jackets.

"You stay there, Troosh. Good boy."

Tim patted the patient dog.

They set off and soon found a gap in the hedge. As they crossed the meadow, Tim's torch beam caught sight of the occasional rabbit scampering away.

"Can we catch one, Dad?"

"I don't see why not. Let's see if we can find their run."

It wasn't long before Sean had found the rabbit run, which seemed in regular use as the grass had been worn away to bare earth. It led up to a small hole in the hedge. Reaching into his pocket he pulled out a coil of wire attached to some twine, and a peg. Forming a loop he placed it over the hole so it was about three inches off the ground. Unravelling the twine he pushed the peg into the ground with his heel. The trap was set.

"OK. Let's go back along the meadow."

They walked quietly along the hedge line one behind the other, slightly stooped, trying to be invisible. It took some twenty five minutes to reach the other side.

"Right, Son, that's far enough, now let's head back towards the snare."

Sean and Tim spread out, kicking the grass to make a disturbance. As they approached their snare they heard frantic scuffling in the undergrowth.

"Sounds like we've caught something, Dad."

Tim spoke with anticipation in his voice. Arriving back at their starting point they knelt down and there before them was a rabbit fighting for all he was worth. Sean reached out and took hold of the rabbit behind the ears; Tim trained his torch forward so his dad could see what he was doing. Lifting the rabbit up by its hind legs, Sean dispatched it with one swift blow. Removing the snare he rolled it up and put it back in his pocket. Tim carried their prize back to the caravan.

Troosh barked; pleased to see their return. Tim got a brew under way while his dad gutted the rabbit, throwing the offal to Troosh, who quickly devoured it. When it was skinned and cleaned he put the rabbit in the pan box under the caravan.

They woke the next morning to find the heavens had opened. It was raining torrents, heavy raindrops bouncing off the roof.

"This sorts the men from the boys." Sean put on his waterproofs. "Seen my wellies, Son?"

"In the cupboard under the cabinet."

"I've got them."

Heading out into the stormy weather Sean got Chalky prepared. The door was open and Troosh dashed inside, stood in the middle of the caravan and shook for all he was worth, splattering Tim in the process.

"Thanks!" Tim reached for a towel to dry his face.

"All set Tim?"

"Yes Dad."

Tim checked that everything was secure before venturing out to join his dad. Holding the reins, he took what shelter he could under the porch. His dad removed the chocks from under the wheels and, stowing them away, he clambered aboard.

"Going to be a hard job finding some dry firewood today." Sean was longing for a brew.

As the rain came crashing down, hitting the outstretched leaves and branches, different sounds could be heard like nature conducting its own symphony. A gusty wind was blowing in all directions. There was no sign of wildlife nor were there any birds flying, but by three o'clock in the afternoon when the clouds started to break, as blue sky appeared, the birds could be heard rejoicing. The warm rays of the sun hitting the road evaporated the rain skywards. Their stomachs were rumbling from the meagre rations that day.

"Will we make it to the farm tonight, Dad?"

"Should be there by seven."

Slowly coming to the top of the hill, Sean pulled Chalky up, for there, laid out before them, was a sight to behold. It was a beautiful valley, with gently rolling hills overlapping on either side and neatly trimmed hedges forming a boundary between the different crops; some short some tall. The low thatched roofs of the white lime-washed cottages were broken at the eves by dormers jutting out. From the chimneys of one or two of the cottages, a plumb of white smoke rose. The mixture of different colours made the scene look like a patchwork quilt.

"That's where we're heading, Son."

Sean pointed to the right at a large farmhouse with numerous outbuildings and cows grazing in one of the fields.

Tim got up from his seat on the porch and went into the caravan, shortly returning with the camera that Joe Maxwell had given him. Looking through the viewfinder he scanned the landscape. Clicking away, he captured the beautiful scene before him.

"Hang on, Dad."

He jumped down and walked a few steps in front of Chalky, turning the camera on his dad.

"Put your cap on."

"Who are you trying to be, Lord Snowdon?" Sean complied with his son's wishes.

"No. David Bailey."

"I might have guessed."

His dad was laughing. Troosh, not wanting to miss out, sat up and looked straight at Tim. Having clicked a few more shots Tim climbed back aboard. They progressed slowly, weaving through the narrow lanes heading down towards the farm. What seemed like a short distance took them more than two hours to cover. Taking a right turn they pulled off the road and went down a long narrow track riddled with bumps and pot holes. What seemed like a picturesque farm from a distance showed definite signs of decay as they approached.

Years of neglect had taken their toll; roof tiles had slipped and lay broken on the ground around the outbuildings, doors ajar clung to their frames by rusting hinges, windows were void of their glass, stinging nettles, four feet high, edged the buildings and the old bales of straw strewn about were being overtaken by the undergrowth.

When they reached the farmhouse they could see its state wasn't much better, but there were signs of life and smoke was coming from the chimney. Bringing the caravan to a halt Sean jumped down. He approached the front door which was more bare wood than what had clearly once been a green high gloss finish. With clenched fist he banged on the door. The whole door and frame shook within the loose brickwork. A dog could be heard barking. Sean took a step back and waited, then tried again, but still no answer, just the dog barking. Turning to Tim he held out his hands and shrugged his shoulders.

"Doesn't look like anyone's home."

"What are we going to do now, Dad?"

Sean looked around for a moment pondering their next move. Then, climbing back aboard, he took the reins and released the brake, slowly turning the caravan around. As they did so a noise could be heard getting closer.

"Listen dad, I can hear something."

Sean pulled on the reins stopping Chalky in his tracks. Even Troosh pricked up his ears. The sound of a tractor could be heard getting ever louder as it got closer. Coming into view it turned into the yard with a trailer hitched to the back. The driver stopped and reached for the key to turn the engine off. With a splutter it fell silent. The man looked curiously at them as he climbed down, as if he wondered who the strangers might be. Sean got down and walked towards him.

"Jacob?"

"That's right." The farmer had a puzzled look on his face.

"It's me, Sean, remember?"

The man, Jacob, squinted as Sean walked towards him. Clearly his eyesight was failing.

"By gad, it is too! Sean! I haven't seen you around these parts for some time."

They shook hands vigorously.

Sean gestured with his arm. "What's happened to the place?"

"It's a sign of the times. Things are bad. Come inside."

"Hang on. I've got my lad with me this time, Jacob." He turned "Tim!" he called.

Tim ran over to join his dad.

"This is my lad, Tim." Sean introduced his son proudly.

"Nice to meet you, Tim,"

"Thank you."

Jacob led the way and they entered the house. They went down the short hallway and into the kitchen. The smell of damp mould and stale pipe smoke hung in the air. There was a double cooking range, once cream in colour now covered in grime, recessed into the chimney breast. Jacob opened one of the doors and threw on a couple of logs. They hissed and crackled as they burst into flames. Closing the door he slid the kettle across onto the hotplate. Sean's eyes scanned the room, taking in the sight of the washing up that had not been done for ages; cups, saucepans and plates piled high in the sink. Food remains had been left on the plates. Inside the pans, mould was growing. Very little light came in through the window by the sink. Months of muck and dust from outside had settled on the pane. Everywhere Sean looked, the once loved home was now neglected. He could see which chair Jacob used. It was the only one that was shiny, just like the seat of his pants. Jacob was searching for three cups, which was no mean feat in the chaotic mess.

"Where's Daisy?" enquired Sean.

Daisy was Jacob's wife and Sean knew that she would never let her home get into such a state.

"She passed away gone four years now. I've lost heart in the place. We had no kids so there's no one to pass it on to,"

There was great sadness in Jacob's voice.

The atmosphere in the room changed. Sean, not knowing what to say, tried to change the subject.

"Nobody else turned up for the potato picking?"

"Haven't done any picking since Daisy been gone."

"Well what do you do then? You must be doing something."

"No, not much. I potter around here and there, still got a few beasts and a few chickens and I can't be bothered with anything else."

Jacob rose to his feet as the kettle came to the boil. Steam belched from the spout. He slid it off the hot plate then seized the cups he had rescued earlier from the sink. He ran them under the tap giving them a shake dry. He then put them on the table. Picking up the brown china teapot he emptied its cold contents into the sink and, opening the window, he chucked out the old teabags. Then having rinsed it out under the tap he threw in three fresh teabags. Filling the teapot with the boiling water he replaced the lid and let it brew. Within a few minutes they were all sitting around the kitchen table talking about old times, with Jacob even managing a smile. Sean explained to Jacob that he had stayed off the road and not travelled, because he wanted to spend more time with his son, and he told him how they had come by the caravan which had led them to have a working holiday and finally arrive at the farm.

Later, Tim and his dad got Chalky settled then fed Troosh. Retrieving the rabbit from the pan box they managed to put together enough for all three of them to have a meal. To finish off, Jacob pulled out an old dusty bottle from the rack in the cupboard. Rubbing his hand over the label he revealed a label that read: *Taylors Finest Port.*

Pulling the cork from the neck of the bottle he took a sniff. "Ah, this will warm the cockles of your heart."

Taking two glasses, Jacob wiped them on his shirt tail, and proceeded to pour two good measures. Raising their glasses the two men toasted each other. Tim stuck to orange squash that he fetched from the caravan. For his dad and Jacob the rest of the night was a blur.

Chapter 10. The great clean-up

The cock crowed early next morning, welcoming in another fine day, but nobody was awake, especially not Sean and Jacob; as, by the time they had finished reminiscing the night before; they had consumed almost two bottles of port. Tim had helped his dad to bed. Stumbling across the yard and falling up the steps of their caravan, Sean had collapsed on his bunk, and, oblivious to anything else, he snored the night away. So a lie in was the order of the day.

When Tim woke, he crept about, for he knew if his dad was woken too early he would be in a grumpy mood after a night on the drink. So, getting dressed, he quietly went outside and, walking over to the farmhouse, he rubbed the glass of the kitchen window. Peering through, he could see Jacob, still where they had left him, sound asleep in his chair.

Taking Troosh, Tim decided to go and explore. He looked in and around the now abandoned and redundant building that once housed pigs and chickens. He found loads of scrap metal that his dad would have been interested in had they had their pick-up. There was machinery just lying about, left where it was last used, overgrown and rusting. Birds had even made a nest in an old seed drill. Coming across an old well, he peered down inside. A rope still hung from the pulley, its bucket gone, probably fallen into the water long ago. The Dutch barn, once standing majestically, was now missing almost all of its corrugated sheeting. Its frame stood naked against the landscape. Tim walked on, heading off into the woods, where he came across an old Anderson shelter used in the war, now half filled with stagnant smelly water. As he walked, the occasional pheasant would take flight with Troosh in hot pursuit. But the birds were safe. They were far too quick for Troosh and the shooting season did not start until the first of October. Coming almost full circle, Tim arrived back in the yard where he was greeted by his dad and Jacob who were sitting on the old timber stand once used for milk churns.

"Fancy a cuppa? The kettle's just boiled," said Jacob.

"No thanks." Tim was thinking about the squalid state of the kitchen. "Maybe later." He did his best to be polite.

Sean finished off his coffee, stood up and stretched.

"See you in a bit, Jacob, I'm going to freshen up. Come on, Tim."

They headed off to their caravan. On entering, Sean poured some cold water into the bowl. Taking his shirt off, he proceeded to have a wash. The coldness of the water and a slight nip in the early morning air soon had him back to normal.

"Dad, how long are we staying here?" Tim was sitting out on the porch, stroking Troosh.

"Well, I've been thinking about that. Maybe we could stay awhile and be of some help to Jacob. He's pretty down and maybe our company would cheer him up. What do you say?"

Tim sat in silence, his hand gliding up and down the dog's back, mulling over what his dad had said. One part of him wanted to get back out on the open road but maybe staying to help would not be such a bad idea.

"Ok Dad, let's stay awhile, but can we sleep in our caravan? I don't much fancy sleeping in that house."

"Sure thing, Son, that house makes me itch a bit, too." Sean dried himself briskly. "I'll go and tell Jacob."

Putting on a clean shirt he headed for the farmhouse, and walked in through the open door.

"Jacob!"

"Up here. I won't be a minute."

Jacob could be heard walking along the landing. Down he came, clumping as he descended, on the threadbare carpet which had worn away to bare floor boards in the middle.

"What can I do for you?"

"I think it is more of what we can do for you."

Sean was rather apprehensive about how to approach the subject without causing offence so he bit the bullet and came straight out with it.

"Jacob we've known each other for many years now, and whenever I stayed with you, your Daisy did me proud."

"What's all this coming to?" quizzed Jacob.

"Well, it seems such a shame to let this place fall apart and you know your Daisy wouldn't be best pleased. So Tim and I thought that it would be a good idea if we stayed on a bit and helped you get the farm going again."

Sean was relieved that he had got that out and he waited for his friend's reply.

"You thought did you?"

Jacob's voice changed. Gripping the back of a chair he looked around as if taking in how he had neglected his home. The silence was deafening. Sean held his breath.

"I........well I suppose you're right. Daisy wouldn't be best pleased, and I have let this place go; and myself."

Sean breathed a sigh of relief, glad it was over and his friend was not offended.

"Where do you suggest we start then, Sean?"

Sean gazed about the kitchen. "Why not here?"

"I Suppose so." Jacob was clearly finding it hard to find any motivation.

Sean went back outside, looking for Tim. He was overcome with relief. He found Tim playing with Troosh.

"Tim..." he called, walking towards him. "I've had a chat with Jacob and he agrees that the place needs sorting out and we can help him, so let's get started."

Returning to the farmhouse they found Jacob in his favourite chair in the kitchen.

"Come on then, let's get cracking."

Sean rolled up his sleeves.

"Fill those pans and the kettle with water and get them on the stove, we need lots of hot water."

Jacob rose from his chair and opened the kitchen window. He collected up the old papers and farming magazines he had amassed over time and threw them all out of the window. He then began collecting up all the faded ragged cushions and heaved them out also. Several cardboard boxes, old egg cartons, an empty wooden orange crate and any number of empty, crushed, cigarette packets followed.

"We'll have a great bonfire later, Lads!"

"That's it; Mate, we'll soon have this place looking like a palace."

Sean set about emptying the overflowing sink. The first kettle was now boiling and Tim had got some washing up liquid from the caravan. Sean, with hot water and a bowl full of suds, washed down the draining boards and surfaces then washed all the plates and crockery. Soon there was a large pile of sparkling dishes on the draining board, Tim was stoking up the range and refilling the pans.

"Got any cloth or rags, Jacob?" Sean looked at him expectantly.

"Will this do?"

Jacob offered up an old bed sheet. Sean ripped it into smaller pieces. Dunking these into the washing up bowl he started to clean the shelves of the cupboards.

"Go and get a tea towel from the caravan please, Tim."

Tim was there and back in a flash and set about drying the dishes and handing them to Jacob to put away.

By the end of the day, the kitchen was just as Sean could remember it; the now mopped floor showing the patterned tiles. Tim had cleaned the windows inside and out. The curtains had been taken down, washed, rinsed and now hung drying in the breeze on the makeshift line tied between the apple trees at the side of the house. But they weren't finished. While the two men continued inside, Tim gathered up all the rubbish which had been thrown out of the window. Taking it well clear of the house, he piled it up, and striking a match, he set the pile alight. More rubbish was now being tossed out of the front door as the other rooms were emptied, ready for cleaning.

Sean, called a halt after a few hours more.

"I think that's enough for one day, what do you say Jacob?"

"You're right there, let's get cleaned up and we can all go down the pub for a pint or two."

All three got themselves ready, Tim checked on their animals before they left. Then they boarded Jacob's pick-up. This was clearly the best that Jacob had felt in a long time. He was smiling and joking as he drove along. Reaching the nearest pub, The Dung Cow, they went inside and enjoyed a pleasant evening of eating, drinking and playing a few games of darts and dominoes. It was after midnight by the time they got home. Sean and Jacob were singing at the tops of their voices and so out of tune it made Tim wince. Jacob went indoors and tripped over his dog. He could be heard cussing as he stumbled upstairs. Tim guided his dad into the caravan and onto his bunk. Then taking off his shoes, he lay too lay down. He had drunk several shandies and felt light headed. Soon he was in the land of nod.

The next day, a couple more hands came to help; local lads they had met in the pub the night before, wanting to earn some extra cash. Mid morning they were all hard at work. Jacob had set the two lads, Tony and Simon, the task of tidying the out houses and collecting up all the scrap metal that was lying around.

By the weekend, after four days of hard graft, the job was complete. The two lads had gone, Jacob had sold all the old scrap and the outdated machinery, and the money had paid everyone's wages and left a tidy sum. Tim had washed and dried all his and his dad's clothes as well.

"Now that we have got you straight I think Tim and me will be on our travels tomorrow," said Sean.

"Couldn't you just stay a bit longer?"

Jacob had grown used to their company.

"The road's calling, Jacob, you know how it is."

"Well, thanks for all that you've done. And you too, Tim. What you've both done is amazing."

That night, they sat in Jacob's kitchen and ate a hearty meal of roast beef with carrots, peas, mashed swede, roast potatoes, and three Yorkshire puddings each. This feast was washed down with a couple of glasses of wine.

Later, Sean and Tim each had a bath, while they had the chance. Tim reflected that he would miss some of the comforts of home as it would now be back to digging a hole behind a bush to go to the toilet.

Next day Sean hitched up Chalky while Tim rounded up the bantams. He also stowed their things away ready for the off.

Jacob came over. "All set?"

"Aye that we are. Well, Jacob, we'll see you some time soon."

Sean cut the conversation short as he wanted to be on his way.

Jacob was holding an envelope in his outstretched hand.

"Here, take this, and I don't want to hear you say no."

There was firmness in his voice.

Sean took the envelope and, folding it in half, he tucked it into his waistcoat pocket.

"Listen," said Jacob, "I phoned Ben Turner, you know, At Hogs Hollow and he's got some raspberry picking, ditching, fencing and other things he needs doing. There's other travellers have already gone down; you'll probably know some of them."

"Sounds great," said Sean.

"And I'll have spuds in for next year, so there'll be potato picking for you and your lad. I'll be expecting you!"

"That's good to hear. You take care now."

Sean grabbed the reins, and with a slap on Chalky's back they were on the move. Jacob stayed rooted to the spot watching until they were out of sight.

Heading back up the lane Sean took the envelope from his waistcoat and handed it to Tim.

"Have a look and see what's in there."

Tim pulled open the flap and peered inside.

"Look, Dad, it's loaded, we're in the money."

He started counting, shuffling the notes between his fingers.

"Eighty five pounds."

"And it's all ours Son, all ours."

"Not bad for nearly a week's work; and we got fed."

Tim got up from the porch and went inside the caravan. Opening the old tobacco jar with the rest of their money in it, he put in the eighty five pounds, then replacing the lid he put the jar back in the bottom drawer.

Hogs Hollow was two days journey across the moors. It was a barren wilderness with the occasional stunted trees forced to lean horizontal in the unrelenting wind. It was all peat bogs, rough grass, heather and gorse bushes. Here and there, a remote house broke this windswept landscape. Sheep roamed freely, grazing on the meagre grass. They wore different coloured dyes on their backs to denote who they belonged to. This was the home of the grouse, a bird that feeds almost entirely on the heather. Grouse are one of the fastest flying birds, highly prized within shooting circles. They would soon need cover; it was almost August the twelfth. The shooting season was about to start.

Chapter 11. Hogs Hollow

When they reached Hogs Hollow, what a sight there was to greet them! In the field before them were a dozen caravans set out in a circle around a large bonfire. Easing Chalky round, they entered the field, Sean standing on the porch and waving as he recognised his fellow travellers. The Smiths were there, and the Whites and the Dyer family. They called out greetings and a crowd assembled around their caravan. Bringing Chalky to a halt, Tim pulled on the brake and Sean jumped down. Tim watched as his dad embraced many strangers who he had not seen before. He knew tonight there would be a great party with loads of food and drink and thick heads in the morning.

By the time darkness fell, everyone was in a merry mood and there was singing and dancing around the camp fire. Tim went round with his dad, being introduced to everyone. He found it hard to remember all their names as there were so many people. He met some lads his own age sitting on benches around a table. They were drinking cans of beer they had acquired and watching the night unfold.

The women were dressed in their finest, their long flowing skirts swirling out as they were swung around by their dancing partners. The fire crackled; embers going up into the night sky to join the twinkling stars. Two trestles were set out with an array of food, everybody just helped themselves. After midnight people started to drift towards their sleeping quarters, some worse for wear, with two steps forward and one step back. Tim made his way back to their caravan alone. His dad was still tripping the light fantastic.

The next morning, as Tim rose and poked his head out of the door, all was quiet. A few women were about, stoking up the fires and putting the kettles on the hook-irons, ready for a brew, but he returned to his bunk and climbed back into his warm sleeping bag. No work today and it was lunch time before the last of the men emerged. People just sat around talking and drinking tea and coffee.

One of the men strode towards them. He spoke commandingly as he passed.

"Sean you're wanted by Ben Turner down in the bottom field."

Ben turner was the farmer and land owner at Hogs Hollow.

"Thanks."

Sean finishing his coffee, got up from the grass, where he had been sitting, and headed off, hands in his pockets and chewing on a blade of grass.

When he reached the bottom field he could not see anyone. He cupped his hands round his mouth to amplify his call.

"Ben Turner?"

"That's me!"

The answering shout came from within a small copse alongside the field.

"Come over here, Sean!"

Sean put one hand on a fence post and vaulted over the fence. He entered the copse. Walking down a well trodden path he came across the farmer filling the feed bins with corn for the young pheasant poults he was rearing.

"Mr. Turner?"

"Call me Ben. So you're Sean. Jacob told me what you did for him."

"Oh it wasn't much and anyway he paid me for the work."

Sean's modesty prevailed.

"Well I'd like you to run the show here for me. I'll make it worth your while."

"I've got my son here with me. We work together."

"Don't worry about him. If he works well I'll pay him too. There's about a fortnight's work, so do we have a deal?"

"I suppose so."

The two men shook hands to seal the deal.

"See you up at the farmhouse in about an hour and we can discuss the details."

Sean duly met up with the farmer who outlined his plans for the next two weeks. After their discussion, Sean headed back to the camp site. When he got to the caravan, Tim was up but looked a bit pale.

"Dad, I feel ill."

Tim was holding his stomach.

"Don't worry, Son, you'll survive."

His dad laughed.

"That'll teach you to drink too much."

Tim got no sympathy.

"Anyway, listen up; I've got some good news. Ben Turner has asked me to run the show here, and I've said yes."

"That's great, Dad, how long is it for?"

"Not long, about a fortnight at most. He's paying both of us and a bonus if all the work gets done."

"A fortnight's OK Dad, but no longer please."

Tim had the travelling bug.

"No longer, Son I promise. I'd best go and get things organised ready for an early start tomorrow."

Sean left the caravan and called a meeting with all the men, outlining the work plan. Nobody had any complaints with Sean taking charge so the delegation of tasks did not take long. The women were put on the soft fruit picking. The men were assigned to do the heavier jobs such as ditching, fence mending and hedge trimming. Sean told the assembled gathering that if all the work was done on time, Ben Turner would throw in some homemade wine for the last night party. This news was met with a cheer from everyone.

The following day, all the men were divided into their teams. In all there were twenty one men and boys so there were three teams of seven. The team that had the ditch clearing job had drawn the short straw for they would be up to their ankles, and sometimes more, in mud, with flies and midges annoying them, while being scratched to bits by hawthorn bushes. The fence mending wasn't too bad, but it did involve a lot of walking around the boundaries as the farm totalled some two hundred acres in all. Tim was put with this team. They had to check all the fence posts, as the cows often rubbed up against them and sometimes snapped them off at ground level. A wrecking bar was used to start the new hole, and then some water was poured in to soften the ground. They placed the new post in the hole upright and using a post thumper with handles on both sides; they beat the new post into position then stapled the wire to it.

The hedge trimming team had a tractor and trailer with a generator on the back. They walked along trimming the new growth, keeping the hedge tight in shape and no more than four feet in height. Another tractor and trailer followed them, with men raking up and loading the cuttings from the hedge.

The women, along with the younger children, worked in-between the long rows of soft fruit. There were raspberries, blackcurrants and strawberries. They picked the soft fruit into punnets and then put the punnets into trays of twelve. These were taken down to the end of each row and stacked, ready for collection. Sean drove a tractor and trailer and went around checking everybody and making sure they were all working. He delivered any materials that were needed, and collected the trays of soft fruit, carefully stacking them on the trailer, then driving back to the farmyard and unloading them inside one of the many barns, ready for collection the next day when they would be taken to market.

Each evening, Sean went to the farmhouse to see Ben Turner and tell him of the day's progress. The weather was good and Ben was pleased with the bumper harvest.

Every day one of the men would stop work early and take a couple of women to the local village where they would buy what provisions were needed for that night's meal. Every one paid in and all the food was shared.

Time went by quickly, and with not a day's rain, progress was good. By day thirteen there was just the tidying up to be done. The massive crop of soft fruit had all been picked and collected and now it was party night. All the old fence posts had been gathered and stacked by the fire, ready. Sean was up at the farmhouse, with Ben Turner, sorting out everybody's money along with Tim. His dad told him the people's names while Tim wrote them on the envelopes, divided the money, put it in and sealed the envelopes.

"Sean," said Ben Turner, "it's been great working with you, and thank you for a job well done. Here's your wages along with your lad's and the bonus I promised."

He passed over a wad of notes. Tim and his dad looked at each other and smiled. Tucking this into his pocket Sean stood up.

"Thanks Ben, we've had a great time."

"Do you fancy having the same job next year?"

"Let's see what next year brings shall we?"

Sean was ever the free spirit.

"Right then. We'd best get this lot down to the others or we might have a mutiny on our hands."

Ben put the envelopes into a box. They left the farmhouse. Tim and his dad carried a case of homemade wine each while Ben carried the wage packets. They drove the short distance to the camp site and stopped inside the enclosure of caravans. Climbing into the back of the pick-up Ben called out each individual's name. Each came forward to receive their wage packets. When everybody had been paid, he made a short speech.

"I'd just like to say a big thank you to everyone here, for all your hard work, sweat and toil. Most of you are familiar faces, with some new, and if you're around next year, look us up. We've always got work to be done. Finally from myself and my wife here's a few bottles of wine for tonight's festivities. I hope you enjoy it."

With that out of the way Ben drove off back to his house. The wine was placed on one of the tables, Sean putting the different varieties together as Tim called the names out. There was parsnip, rhubarb, potato, elderberry and raspberry. Another man went round with a cap, collecting money from everyone to make a kitty for food and drink for the evening. Some of the women had spent most of the day baking.

The trestle tables were covered in festive red tablecloths. Once the supplies had been fetched from the village, all the drink, food and baking was laid out. The old fence posts were now well alight. Everybody had washed and dressed in their best, men in colourful waistcoats, red neckerchiefs and flat caps; Woman in bright skirts with shawls around their shoulders and clattering bangles on their wrists. They all tucked into the food. There was plenty for everyone. Bottles of beer were opened, wine was passed around and the singing and dancing began with music provided by fiddle players.

Tim began talking to one of the girls who he had got to know during the last fortnight. Her name was Maria. They sat on the grass round the back of the caravans, leaning against a log, just chatting and staring up into the night sky and listening to the music. Suddenly, for no reason, she leaned forward and kissed him. Tim remained motionless for he had never been kissed by a girl before and didn't know what to do next.

"What's up?"

She looked into his face.

"Er...I um...ah..."

"You sure you're all right? Didn't you like it?"

"Yes, it was kind of... nice."

"Only nice? Shall I do it again and see if you like it more?"

"I think we should go and join the others."

Tim jumped to his feet. Maria got to her feet and brushed the grass from her skirt. She stroked Tim's face. She appeared to realise how bashful he was. They spent the rest of the evening dancing but Tim kept Maria at arm's length.

It was gone midnight, the full moon high in the night sky, casting faint shadows on the ground. The fire was all but out. People headed back to their caravans, the singing was now just a murmur from one or two voices. Tim found his dad and helped him back to their caravan. It was a struggle. His dad had his arm round Tim's shoulder, and it was two steps forward two steps sideways and one step backwards but they made it eventually.

Tim sat his dad down on the steps, went inside and got the bunk ready. Helping his dad up the steps, he sat him down on the edge of the bunk and then, as if in slow motion his dad fell backwards. His head missed the pillow and hit the woodwork with a thump. Sean gave out a moan but didn't wake up. He just started to snore. Tim took off his boots and threw a blanket over him before settling himself down for the night.

Morning came and Tim rose, opening the door. The early mist was rising over the fields. The cinders were smouldering in the camp fire, still giving off enough heat to boil the overhanging kettles. The clatter of pots could be heard as the women started packing away their belongings, Tim turned as he heard his dad stir.

"What time is it?" Sean sat up, and rubbed his eyes.

Tim glanced across at the clock on the wall.

"Five past nine."

"Best get a wash then."

Tim trudged over to the stand pipe with his bucket. As he approached he saw Maria, who had just finished filling her pail.

"Good morning," she said in a coy voice.

"Oh, hello."

"Did you sleep well?"

"Fine, no problem. Did you?"

"Oh, I slept very well."

Tim hurriedly put his bucket down and turned on the tap, wishing the water would come out faster so he could get away.

"So where are you going from here, Tim?"

"Don't know yet. Where are you heading?"

"Down country for the apple picking. You fancy coming along?"

"I think Dad's got plans."

He picked up the bucket, splashing the water from it as he almost ran back to the caravan. Maria was beautiful. There was something about her. She intrigued him. Taking the steps two at a time he burst into the caravan.

"Where's the fire?" exclaimed his dad.

"I had to get away from.......her!"

Tim glanced outside. Maria was still standing near the tap, gazing over at him. His dad stood up to have a look outside.

"Hmm, I like your taste in girls," he said laughing.

"Thanks for nothing, Dad."

Tim poured the water into the bowl. His thoughts were all over the place. He had never felt like this before

It was midday. They had all eaten together; everybody had mucked in picking up all the rubbish; what could be burnt was put on the fire and the rest bagged up and left in a neat pile. Chalky now stood ready to go after his fortnight's rest, and Sean and Tim were waving their goodbyes. Tim gazed around the field looking for Maria. On seeing her he stood up on the porch with his cap in hand and waved. She returned the wave then blew him a kiss. He sat back down blushing. He smiled to himself. His dad watched the proceedings.

"Young love," he murmured.

Back on the open road, the afternoon passed quickly. On the stroke of six o'clock, with the church bells pealing, they pulled off the road on the outskirts of a small village called Picklewickie. It was a cluster of maybe a dozen houses and a pub by the village green.

"Come on, Son, no cooking tonight, let's get Chalky pegged out and we'll head for the pub."

Tim didn't needed to be asked twice. A good meal and no washing up was great. Before the church clock had struck seven they were both walking in through the front door of The

Dog and Duck, a small quaint place with low ceilings, smoke stained paintwork and horse brasses nailed to the beam over the fire place.

"Alright for my lad to sit in here?"

"No problem, make yourself at home."

The man behind the bar was affable and left off drying glasses to attend to them.

"A pint of bitter, and a shandy for the lad, please."

The barman pulled on the tall black handle. The bitter coming out of the nozzle swirled around in the pint glass, topped off with a frothy head.

"What's cooking tonight?" Sean asked.

"I'll fetch you a menu."

The barman placed their drinks on the bar and reached alongside the till to pull out a menu card. Sean tucked this under his arm, picked up the drinks and returned to where Tim now sat. Putting the drinks down, he passed the menu to Tim.

"Right, what are we going to have?"

"Lets see, there's a choice of chicken, cod in batter, jumbo sausage, scampi or pizza all served with chips and peas,"

Tim read the menu to his dad.

"It all sounds good. I'm going to have the chicken. What do you fancy, Son?"

"Pizza please, Dad."

They ordered their meal, and, before long, it was being served to their table, on white china plates with a salad garnish on the side, their knives and forks wrapped up in red serviettes. They tucked in and followed this with two banana splits, washed down with one more drink each, before bidding their farewells and heading back to their caravan. Night had fallen. You could see the stars for it was a fine night and the full moon lit their way. Sean put his arm round his son's shoulders. Looking down he gave him a squeeze. They had grown very close, and though they didn't always see eye to eye there was never any real upsets.

"It sure is a fine night."

"Sure is, Dad, and great to be free as a bird and go where ever we please."

Before retiring to their bunks they checked on Chalky, gave the bantams some corn in their cage and fed Troosh.

"Good Night, Dad."

" 'Night, Son."

That night they slept soundly in their bunks, well fed and happy.

At seven thirty, Sean was opening the top door to let in the rays of sunlight. He kicked Tim's bunk.

"Come on, sleepy head."

Tim sat up, rubbing his eyes. Then, climbing out of his sleeping bag he stood up, looking over his dad's shoulder to peer outside. Chalky was enjoying the sunshine and having a good roll in the grass. Sean slipped the bolt and opened the bottom door to let Troosh out. The dog jumped down and had a good sniff around. Spying a rabbit he started barking and gave chase. Tim and his dad washed and got dressed, folded the bunks away and had breakfast of bread and jam and a mug of tea. Troosh came back panting and out of breath, for his quarry had eluded him. Tim filled his bowl with water and Troosh lapped it up.

The next few days were spent meandering along the country lanes, taking in the sights.

"We need to camp up somewhere by a stream for a couple of days to catch up on some washing and things."

"OK, Dad, do you have somewhere in mind?"

"Aye, not too far from here, and we could do some rabbiting."

"Sounds great."

So the next couple of days were spent washing and drying their clothes over gorse bushes. They gave Chalky a good brush down too and they topped up their supplies and collected fire wood. And Tim became quite accomplished at setting snares.

Chapter 12. Boys in blue

Eventually they headed for one of Sean's old stops, the Appleton place. It was another fair day and the traffic was light as Chalky sauntered along.

"Dad, if we get chance, I need some more films for my camera because I want to show Joe everywhere we've been when we get home."

"First chance we get, we'll stop off."

Tim stood up. "Fancy a drink of orange, Dad?"

"Just the job."

Tim went into the caravan and made them both a drink, filling the glasses half full so as not to spill any while they were going along.

"Thanks, Son.,

Sean took his glass.

Tim sat back down and watched the world go by, enjoying every moment. Just then Chalky's ears pricked up and he stopped. A flash of brown flew across the road in front of them, then another and then more, just ten feet away. It was a small herd of roe deer. A majestic stag brought up the rear. Seeing his harem had crossed the road safely he glanced in their direction before following on. They went on their way.

It was three thirty in the afternoon, before Sean spoke.

"Almost there, Son."

"Good, my bum's getting sore!"

The Appleton place was just off the main road. Sean guided Chalky onto a patch of grass and pulled up and Tim jumped down and put the chocks under the wheels.

"Stay there, Tim, I won't be long."

Sean crossed the road. The caravan was soon out of view as he went down a beech-lined driveway towards the house. He went round the back of the house and knocked on the door. Out from one of the sheds came a collie, barking, followed by its owner.

"Yes, can I help you?"

The man looked Sean up and down.

"I'm looking for Mr. Appleton."

"Ah. He's my father in law. Well I'm sorry to inform you but he's in hospital, had a heart attack. I'm running the place now."

"I'm sorry to hear that. I've come to see if there's any work."

"Sorry once again. We're all mechanized now. We don't use casual labour."

"Do you have anything for a couple of days? I don't mind what it is."

"I wish I could help you but there's nothing at all."

"Well, thanks anyway. Goodbye."

Sean headed back to the caravan. Crossing the road he climbed aboard. Tim released the chocks and joined him.

"Any luck?"

He already knew the answer, just by looking at his dad's face.

"Not this time Son, so let's look for a camp site."

It was a good hour before they found a spot with grazing for Chalky. A stream ran nearby. They pulled far enough off the road so as not to draw attention to themselves. While Sean took care of the horse, Tim gathered up some stones to make a ring around the camp fire then collected firewood. Starting the fire, Tim banged in the hook-iron then filled the kettle from the stream ready to make a brew. After eating, they sat chatting. Sean regaled Tim with more stories of his travels with Jim and some of the antics they got up to. They spoke of what they would do next and where they would go. In the firelight Tim told his dad that he was having the time of his life and never wanted it to end.

They carried on travelling and over the next few days they tried several more places for work but there was nothing doing. Most of the farmers now had machines to do the work. So on they went. There was no rush. Time was on their side. Tim, now an accomplished driver, took over the reins more and more

One day, when Tim was driving, a police car overtook them. The blue and white Ford Anglia pulled up in front with its blue revolving light flashing and the STOP sign illuminated. A tall police officer got out from the passenger side.

"Pull over.,

He indicated a gravel lay-by.

"I'll take the reins. Go ahead Chalky."

Sean guided the horse off the road and pulled up. The second officer got out of the car.

"What's the problem, Officer?"

"Well now, there's been a few problems in these parts lately and we're just continuing our enquires."

"That's it, see a couple of travellers on the road and think they'll do."

"Now it's not like that."

It was the taller of the two policemen who spoke.

"I'm sure." Remarked Sean.

Taking a notebook from his pocket the other officer gave Sean a meaningful look.

"Can you tell me your movements and whereabouts these past few days?"

"You seem to know what goes on. You tell me."

Sean's snappish tone was due to the fact that he was becoming annoyed by this for he had little time for the law. He had been arrested a few times in the past for getting into fights with his brother and being drunk and disorderly.

"Now, we can either do this here or we can go down the nick. It's your choice."

Impatience was apparent in the policeman's tone also.

"Dad, Dad, let's just tell them what they want to know," pleaded Tim.

"OK let's do it here."

While the policeman asked Sean and Tim more questions his tall colleague was giving the outside of the caravan the once over; opening up the boxes on the underside and at the back. He found nothing to interest him. With all the questions answered, the other policeman returned his notebook to his pocket.

"Mind if we look inside?"

"Do we have a choice?"

Sean now sharp with his words.

Tim jumped down.

"Troosh, here!"

Troosh, snarling, came to heel. The tall policeman climbed up and entered the caravan. Systematically he went through all the drawers and cupboards, pulling the books off the shelves and turning their bedding upside down.

"Nothing here."

He climbed back down.

"OK, let's call it a day," said the other one and they headed for their car.

"Hey, just a minute," shouted Sean, "You can't leave our caravan like this!"

"Can't we? Just watch us."

They got into their car and slammed the doors. Troosh took a flying leap and jumped up at the driver's door, pawing at the glass, barking. The two officers looked shaken. The driver fumbled with the keys before starting the engine and driving off.

"Well, Son, we'd best get this lot sorted out."

"Dad, maybe if you hadn't wound them up so much, they wouldn't have done this."

"Could be worse, Tim.,Back years ago we were always being hounded by the police, never any peace no matter where we went. Trouble was, some of the travellers did get up to no good, so we all got tarred with the same brush."

"I'm glad to see the back of them," said Tim.

They continued on their way late into the evening before finding a place to stop and make camp. The weather had taken a turn for the worse. The wind had got up and there was heavy rain. Sean tethered Chalky and clambered back inside, Tim had got the queenie stove going. Filling the kettle he put it on the top.

"Right, let's see what we can find to eat."

"Not much, Dad."

"We can rustle something up I'm sure."

Getting the smaller of the two frying pans out, Sean placed it on the stove.

"Now, let's see...a few boiled spuds left over and those cooked carrots we didn't finish - that can all go in... and two tomatoes as well. Take that spoon Tim and start stirring it round, I'll nip outside and get that bit of cooked rabbit from the cold box."

Sean was soon back; slicing off the meat from the carcass and sharing it out between two plates, tossing the bones to Troosh to devour.

"Almost done Dad, it's just starting to go crispy and brown."

"Good. I'll make the tea and butter the bread. You serve it up."

Tim spooned out their supper, and they both sat down on his dad's bunk and tucked in with relish, finishing off by wiping their bread around their plates.

"Where can you get better grub than that?"

"Nowhere, Dad, that was great, I'm stuffed."

They finished drinking their tea. Sean collected their plates and put them out on the porch so the rain could do the washing up.

"I think we should be making tracks for home tomorrow, see how your Uncle Jim has been coping. What do you say?"

"I don't want to, but I suppose we have to sometime and now is as good a time as any."

Tim was pleased that his dad had consulted him.

"All right that settles it. Tomorrow it is."

"How long will it take us Dad?"

"About eight to ten days. Anyway let's hit the sack."

The weather had not let up at all, that day. The wind was still howling, and heavy rain beat against the side of the caravan which was rocking with every gust of wind. But inside, Tim and his dad were snug and warm as they settled down for the night.

Tim was woken by Troosh, pawing at his sleeping bag wanting to be let out. Sliding from his sleeping bag, Tim released the catch on the door, letting Troosh escape. Though the wind had subsided, the rain had not let up at all. Tim quickly shut the door and snuggled back in the warm. He must have dozed back to sleep for the next thing he knew was his dad nudging him to say he had made the tea.

"Morning Son, sleep well?"

"Fine thanks Dad."

He sat up and took his cup.

"Autumn's here and winter is just around the corner with the trees lowering their flags."

"What Dad?"

"That's what we call it. It's an old saying, when the trees lose their leaves."

"Oh."

Tim sipped his tea.

Taking the lid off the stove, Sean toasted some bread for their breakfast. After this they made ready and began the long trip home, stopping off now and again to replenish their larder.

By early afternoon of the third day, they were sauntering along on with the sun to the back of them. The air was full of a smell of coal and steam and as they progressed the smell got stronger. Rounding a bend in the road they saw that ahead of them was a steam traction engine, belching smoke from its funnel. It was towing a caravan and a dismantled fairground ride. Staying back a safe distance, so as not to get covered in soot, they followed. After a few miles, the traction engine pulled off the road and into a field. By now it was evening. They could see that there were more traction engines in the field.

"Dad, can we join them?"

"I Suppose so. Come on Chalky."

With a slight quickening of pace Chalky pulled their caravan over the grass verge and into the field. Heading towards the gathering of people Sean enquired if it was alright to camp there for the night. One of the men indicated for Sean to pull over to the left side of the field along with the other caravans. Tapping the side of his flat cap as a thank you gesture, Sean steered Chalky to their pitch for the night. Unhitching the horse, Sean staked him out. Tim let out the bantams so they could stretch their legs.

Once he had collected the eggs, he went inside and got the stove going. He put the small frying pan on. Cutting a knob of lard from the packet he flicked it into the pan. As it warmed it drifted round the pan with a sizzle. Sean returned, pleased to see Tim preparing their tea. Using all the eggs he had collected from the previous couple of days, Tim cracked six into the pan. As the whites of the eggs started to appear Sean cut four slices of bread layered them with a good helping of butter and placed them on the plates. Tim removed the frying pan and Sean put the kettle on the top of the stove. Tim loaded two of the pieces of bread with three eggs each. Taking a knife he broke into the yolks and spread them around, sprinkling on salt and pepper then he put the other pieces of bread on. He handed one of the sandwiches to his dad and they both sat out on the porch and tucked into their meal. Tim took a large bite as the mixture of egg yolk and butter dribbled down his chin. They threw their crusts to Troosh. Sean took the empty plates and set about making the tea, rejoining Tim to drink it. They watched the fairground people go about their business unloading and setting up their rides and stalls.

The men and women worked as a team, erecting the side show stalls. There was a shooting range with pellet guns, a tin can alley with hard canvas balls to throw, and a coconut shy with the coconuts perched on tall, red and white painted stands. There were small glass bowls set out in rows where you had to get a ping pong ball inside to win a goldfish and playing cards pinned on a large board where you had to score twenty-one or more to win a prize. One was a circular stall standing all on its own with a candy floss machine inside.

Tim and his dad took a stroll, and soon joined in to lend a helping hand; grabbing armfuls of coco mats and taking them over to the helter skelter. Tim was invited to try out the ride. Going in through the doorway he climbed the wooden staircase to the top. Positioning his mat carefully, he jumped on and with arms in the air he flew round and round as he went down, coming to rest at the bottom. Then it was across to the swing boats and they helped to lift them up to be bolted onto their steel rods. There was a nostalgic atmosphere of days gone by. The most splendid ride took centre stage; the galloping horses, where brightly painted, carved wooden horses, trimmed with gold, went round and round, rising and sinking on their shiny brass poles. High above all the other rides rose The Big Wheel.

Tim looked round to see the traction engine fired up and heading in his direction. It gave a couple of blasts from its whistle and people stood aside as it trundled along on its rubber rimmed wheels. He could see it better up close. It was a Burrell Showman's Road Locomotive, splendid in crimson with highly polished brass. Getting into position the driver disengaged the gears. On the front was an extension over the smoke box. This had a large dynamo mounted on the top. The men had already laid out the cables and then connected them to the dynamo. Sliding the drive belt over the fly wheel and the pulley, the driver pulled some levers and the dynamo hummed into action. First the lights around the canopy burst into life and then the whole fairground lit up. There were two other generators to help with all the power required.

Tim could soon smell food. The burger and hot dog stand was now bathed in light, the hot plates laden with meat.

Everyone started to gather round. All the work was done. They were ready to receive paying customers the next day. Tim and his dad were made most welcome and, joining the queue, they had their fill. They stayed until lunch time the next day. Before leaving Tim tried out all the rides and his final job was helping to bag up the goldfish ready to be given as prizes.

Chapter 13. Familiar surroundings

As they arrived back among familiar surroundings, friends tooted their horns as they passed, welcoming them back. Turning off the main road, they went along the lane towards Waltonson village and, soon after, they were making their way up the track to Dunroamin. On reaching the gate, Tim jumped down to open it and Sean drove through. Tim secured the gate and Troosh leapt out and began chasing the cats and sending them to ground.

"Whoa!"

Sean pulled on the reins bringing Chalky to a halt.

"OK, Tim, put the chocks under the wheels and I'll unharness Chalky."

Their place was quiet. The animals all seemed fine. Sean released Chalky and walked him over to his paddock. Swinging the five bar gate open, he removed Chalky's halter and let him go. Closing the gate he stood for a while just watching the horse running around kicking his hind legs in the air and shaking his head.

"There you go, Chalky, you can have a nice long rest now."

Meanwhile, Tim was heading for their caravan, lifting up the concrete block by the front door to reveal their key. He unlocked the door and went inside. It smelt musty after being shut up for weeks so he opened the windows to give it a blow through. Sean came in clutching provisions left from their travels and placed them on the table.

"Well, home again Son, back to normal."

"Yes, worse luck."

"Come on, things are not that bad and we can always hit the road together next summer."

"Do you mean that, Dad?"

"Sure thing! Now, let's get organised here so we can get an early night."

They didn't bother to empty anything else out of their caravan, just shut the door and left it. Having a quick wash they both hit the sack and slept like logs.

Troosh was going mad the next morning. Tim just turned over and buried his head under the pillow so it was left to his dad to see what all the commotion was. He opened the door to see Troosh straining on his wire. It was Jim and Sonny.

"Good morning, Jim! Come in... come in. How do, Sonny."

"Good Morning!"

They stepped in through the door way, beam

"Go and stick the kettle on, Jim; I'll just get some clothes on."

As he passed Tim's bedroom, Sean gave the sliding door a kick.

"Come on, Tim. Rise and shine! Jim and Sonny are here."

Sean, Jim and Sonny were sitting at the table drinking tea when Tim came through, tugging the cord tight on his dressing gown.

"Morning, All," he greeted them.

"What time did you get back?" asked Jim

"Early evening," answered Sean.

As they sat round the table, Tim and his dad recounted their adventures on the road. Sean told Jim who they had met up with at Ben Turner's place and didn't miss out the story about a certain girl named Maria who had fancied Tim. That brought a chuckle from everyone and made Tim go red in the face.

Jim was sorry to hear about Mr. Appleton in hospital with a heart attack because he had been going to his place each year for a long time. Sean explained how his son in law now had machines to do the work. And he told them of poor old Daisy who had died and how they had helped Jacob get his place going again.

"Sounds like you both had a great time but it's time we made a move. Come on, Sonny. I'll catch up with you later, Sean."

Jim rose to his feet.

"Thanks again, Jim, for watching the place for us. Come on Tim we'd best get a move on and get ourselves organised. The animals won't feed themselves."

By late morning, most of the chores were finished. Tim was just filling the pail with corn to scatter for the chickens, while Sean, wielding the hose pipe, was topping up the water trough for the pigs. They put in some fresh bedding then all was done.

"Fancy going out later? We need to do some shopping and we can drop off your films to be developed at the same time,"

"Yeah sure, Dad."

"Firstly though, we need to empty the caravan and get it back under cover. I'll fetch the pick-up; you go and get some rope."

Tim did as he was asked. His dad reversed the pick-up into position, then got out and dropped the tail gate.

"Right, Tim, you lift up the shafts and I'll back up to you."

Holding the driver's door open he leaned out so he could watch where he was going. Carefully he edged back. The shafts began to slide inside the back of the truck.

"Stop!"

The shafts were just touching the bulkhead. Getting out, Sean took the rope and tied it to the front axle of the caravan and then to the tow hitch of the pick-up.

"Clear those old pallets out of the way, Tim."

He jumped back into the pick-up. Tim shifted the pallets and slowly Sean edged the pick up forward. Right hand down a bit he headed out into the compound, then, straightening up, he came to a halt.

"OK, Tim, watch me as I go back."

With the handbrake off, Sean edged backwards, easing the caravan undercover.

"Almost there, Dad, steady as you go."

Tim raised his hand.

"Steady... steady, OK that's it, STOP!"

Sean applied the brakes then got out. Tim put the chocks under the front wheels of the caravan. Untying the rope Sean threw it into the back of the pick-up and they lifted the shafts out, raising them up in the air until they came to rest against the top of the porch. Sean drove out.

"We can lift her up later and put her on some chocks to take the weight off the springs to overwinter. Come on, Son, let's get cleaned up and we can go into the village."

Their first port of call was the general store. Into the back of the pick-up went four boxes of provisions then round to the butchers to see Mick again, regaling him with tales of their travels. They left with some chops, bacon and, Tim's favourite, some belly pork. He was looking forward to it cooked in the pan and then sprinkled with brown sugar and put under the grill. He could almost taste it.

Across the road they went, and into the chemist's. Tim opened the door and the brass bell above it rang. Going up to the counter he placed his six films on the glass top. He still had one in his camera, not quite finished. The woman behind the counter gave him receipts for each film, and told him they would be ready the following week.

Last stop before home was to call into Joe Maxwell's. Pulling up outside, half on the pavement and half on the road, they got out. Joe was not in the front shop so they walked around the back to the workshop. They were greeted by rhythmical banging and there was Joe, down in the pit under a Rover, with hammer and chisel in hand, trying to loosen a nut and bolt.

"What do you have to do to get some service around here?"

Sean leaned against the door.

"Well I'll be....you old son of a gun!"

Joe came out of the pit two steps at a time, extending his arm to shake hands then wiping the sweat from his brow.

"Good to see you both again. I thought I might have to find somebody else to take my scrap away. Anyway how was it then? Did you enjoy it? What was the weather like? Where did you go? What did you get up to?"

Joe fired off so many questions at once that they couldn't get a word in.

"It was great. I didn't realise how much I missed being out on the road." Said Sean.

"And you?"

Joe turned towards Tim.

"It was fantastic, Joe. I've got some great pictures to show you when I get them back."

"Come on, let's have a cuppa and you can tell me more."

Joe led the way inside. The afternoon passed by before they knew it, and that evening, back home, Tim and his dad sat talking well into the night, contentedly planning their next year's travels.

Roy Young was born in 1951 in Hamble, Hampshire. He was brought up in the country side and lived in Old Bursledon for a number of years. At the age of twelve he started to work part time on the land and as a gardener, and met and befriended a number of travellers. Throughout his teens he worked on the land and on building sites, and was taught some of the old country crafts and customs by his grandparents and the local gamekeeper. Later he joined the navy and travelled for a few years seeing other cultures before settling down and getting married. After gaining more experience in the building industry Roy went into teaching, becoming a further education lecturer at local colleges. Now, after a spell running his own business, he is a manager with a large local construction company.

Printed in Great Britain
by Amazon

20595998R00068